He watched her.

With a flash of insight Jamie realised that he was in great danger of becoming the noble and untouchable widower in Sarah's eyes. And he did not want her to think of him as untouchable, he realised. That was the last thing on his mind.

So he could now do one of two things. He could politely take his leave of her. Thank her for the sherry and head for the door.

Or he could kiss her.

Sharon Kendrick had a variety of jobs before training as a nurse and a medical secretary, and found that she enjoyed working in a caring environment. She was encouraged to write by her doctor husband after the birth of their two children and much of her medical information comes from him and from friends. She lives in Surrey where her husband is a GP. She has previously written medical romances as Sharon Wirdnam and now, as Sharon Kendrick, she divides her time between the medical and modern romances.

TAKING
IT ALL

BY
SHARON KENDRICK

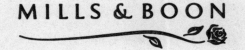

MILLS & BOON

To my gorgeous son, Patrick,
who is the best boy in the world.

*MILLS & BOON, the Rose Device and
LOVE ON CALL are trademarks of the publisher.
Harlequin Mills & Boon Limited,
Eton House, 18-24 Paradise Road, Richmond, Surrey TW9 1SR*

© Sharon Kendrick 1996

ISBN 0 263 79857 7

*Set in Times 11 on 12$^{1}/_{2}$ pt. by
Rowland Phototypesetting Limited
Bury St Edmunds, Suffolk*

03-9610-41369

Made and printed in Great Britain

CHAPTER ONE

'OK. No, REALLY. No. It can't be helped.' Now, how the *hell* was he going to explain this to Harriet?

Jamie Brennan replaced the telephone receiver with a resigned sigh and turned to face his daughter, realising as he looked down at her that an explanation was going to be unnecessary in any case. Harriet might be only nine years old but she knew her father inside out!

Her face took on the belligerent expression that seemed to be growing more and more familiar these days. 'You're not going into the hospital *again*, are you, Daddy?' she demanded querulously.

'It's a case of having to, Harriet,' said Jamie ruefully. 'I'd much rather stay here with you. You know that.'

'But it's Saturday! And you *promised* to take me swimming!' Harriet accused hotly, disappointment making her rosebud mouth tremble with threatened tears.

Jamie shook his dark head. He needed to be firm on this one. 'No, sweetheart, I didn't actually *promise*. Daddy doesn't make promises if he knows that he might not be able to keep them. What I actually said was that if it was quiet on the wards then we would go swimming. The trouble is that it's been very busy. When a baby decides it's time to enter the world it doesn't give a monkey's what time of the day or night it is!'

She didn't respond to the joke but kept uncharacteristically silent. He looked at her bent head, at the strawberry-blonde hair plaited into two thick braids which made her look so appealingly old-fashioned and his heart contracted with love.

'I'm sorry, sweetheart.' He made a placatory move towards her but her skinny arm flailed him away and he recognised the gesture for what it was—defensiveness, rather than aggression. 'Listen, Harriet,' he explained patiently. 'A woman has just been admitted to the labour ward. They need me there.' He didn't burden her with the fact that his senior registrar was away on holiday and that the new registrar didn't seem to be shaping up as expected. Consequently, even more of the workload had fallen on Jamie's shoulders than usual.

Harriet turned candid brown eyes up at him. 'Why can't one of the other doctors do it?'

'Because I'm the consultant and ultimately I'm responsible for what goes on in my department,' he replied slowly. 'It's a difficult case and I have to oversee what the registrar is doing. He's still fairly new.' But he could see that his appeal carried little weight—the cares of the obstetrics and gynaecological unit mattered little to a child who had already lost more than any child should ever be expected to lose. And Harriet Brennan had been just four years old when her mother had died. . .

'But I wanted to go swimming!' objected Harriet sulkily.

'And so did I,' said Jamie gently. 'Very much. But you can still go swimming. Marianne can take you.' He smiled. 'And she's a much better swimmer than me!'

'I don't *want* Marianne to take me!' said Harriet, screwing up her nose. 'I want *you*!'

Jamie did a rapid mental calculation. If the patient needed a drip to speed up her contractions, as he suspected she would, then that would give him a few hours' grace while they watched to see if it worked. And, provided that there were no complications, then he *could* be out of the labour ward in time to take Harriet swimming. Just.

'Tell you what,' he said appeasingly. 'If everything goes according to plan and everyone is happy then I'll drive straight from the hospital to the swimming pool and meet you and Marianne there. But I'm not promising, sweetheart; things may crop up—you know how it is.'

Harriet pulled a face. She sure did. Like every doctor's daughter in the world she had learned never to rely on Daddy being there.

'OK?' prompted Jamie and gave a grin which made him look much younger than his thirty-three years.

Harriet nodded, mollified. She adored her father and since the death of her mother was understandably closer to him than a lot of children of her age would have been. 'OK,' she grinned back.

'Right!' His domestic problems settled, Jamie automatically swung into his professional persona. 'Marianne!' he called, as he glanced quickly into the mirror to see if he was presentable enough to appear on the wards and then grimaced. He was most definitely *not* presentable!

He had been sawing through a diseased apple branch in the orchard and his face had smudges of dust adorning it, while his hair was completely rumpled. Add to that the dark shadows beneath his eyes, incurred from a difficult breech delivery he had had to do in the early hours, and he looked as though he had been up at a party all night. When was the last time he had been to a party—all night or otherwise? he wondered just a touch longingly.

He would need to wash up before he left for the hospital. 'Marianne!' he called again, as he pulled a comb from his back pocket and raked it through his thick, brown-black hair.

'Coming!' came the yelled reply and Marianne loped into the room with all the careless grace of an eighteen-year-old.

Jamie had had a tough job finding a nanny to suit Harriet and him. He had interviewed several young women in their early twenties—all extremely well qualified, it had to be admitted— but who all seemed to find the prospect of working for a youngish, successful widower doctor apparently irresistible. Jamie had never been what could have been described as a rake—he had married young and had loved his wife very much—but, even so, he could recognise a come-on when he saw one.

And the very idea of having someone looking after his daughter who made it patently clear that she was sexually attracted to *him*—well, frankly, it appalled him.

He was also human enough to admit to himself the potential for danger if he had a strapping blonde stunner living so closely with them! He was a man, not a robot, and he had not slept with a woman for a very long time. Not since his wife had died, in fact.

He gave a small self-deprecating smile as he realised how falsely noble this made him sound! Because there *had* been a woman that he had grown very fond of—the lovely Verity—but the relationship had never become sexual because Verity had still been in love with the father of her child. The experience had made Jamie wary and he had thrown himself into his work and his research and into being a good father and had pushed the thought of women to the back of his mind.

But lately. . .

Lately he had felt his senses clamour to be allowed to live again. So far he had repressed the desire but introducing a Junoesque Swede into his home, with legs all the way up to her armpits, was just *asking* for trouble!

As a kind of reaction to this, Jamie had then set about finding a kind and motherly figure to care for Harriet when he wasn't around. He had been able to picture the applicant quite clearly—in his mind's eye she always seemed to be wearing a floral pinny! He had had images of the scent of apple pie drifting in from the kitchen and clean washing billowing on the line, while Harriet would happily assist the matronly paragon to accomplish all these domestic chores!

It had been Harriet herself who had pointed out that the older women who were arriving for interviews were hardly likely to want to take her swimming, ice-skating or walking miles with Blue, her dog.

Jamie had had to agree with her and had just been getting desperate when the professor of medicine at Southbury Hospital had come to his rescue. He had a daughter aged eighteen, who was resitting her A levels. She was active, fun, adored children and needed a job before going up to university the following September. Jamie had met her the following day and had been convinced that she was just the kind of carer he was looking for for Harriet.

And he had been right. Marianne had fitted into Jamie's and Harriet's lives like a dream; she was more like an older sister to Harriet than a nanny. In fact, the year was almost up. In September Marianne would be off to Durham University, which left Jamie with only the summer holidays to find her replacement. He stifled a sigh, dreading the prospect.

What must it be like, he wondered fleetingly, to have the kind of normal family life that most couples took for granted? But he banished the thought with his usual resilience and humour.

He turned to Marianne with a smile. 'How's your crawl these days?'

Marianne, too, was a doctor's daughter. She pulled a conspiratorial face at Harriet, then affected an expression of mock surprise. 'Don't tell me!' she exclaimed dramatically. 'Daddy can't go swimming—he's got to work!'

'Yes!' pouted Harriet.

'Bet he's fibbing,' Marianne hissed, out of the side of her mouth. 'He probably got Sister to bleep him as an excuse. He's feeling too lazy and middle-aged to go swimming!'

'Hey! Less of the "middle-aged"!' protested Jamie with a grin. 'I have to go in and oversee a delay in labour,' he explained succinctly. 'But, provided nothing else crops up, I'll come straight to the pool. How's that?'

'Only if you promise to race us,' challenged Marianne, with a wink at her young charge.

Jamie was as competitive as the next man. He also had the so-far-undisclosed memory of winning the county challenge cup for swimming. It might be time to show his daughter a glimpse of what her dad *used* to be like—before work and life had eaten up every waking hour! 'Sure,' he said innocently, 'I'll give you a race.' Then he gave a deliberately worried frown and he had to bite his lip as he saw Marianne and Harriet exchange concerned glances.

'Don't worry—we'll give you a head start,' said

Marianne kindly, and Jamie had to turn away to hide his smile as he headed off to wash his face and hands before driving to the hospital.

'This is it!' exclaimed the nurse cheerfully. 'Bit small—but the view makes up for it!'

'Thanks for showing me here,' replied Sarah with a smile.

'Don't mention it!' said the nurse cheerfully. 'That's what neighbours are for! I live just two doors down, if you're interested.'

'Thanks,' said Sarah rather absently, depositing her battered suitcase on the floor of the small flat and raking a hand back through the abundance of dark hair that spilled over her shoulders. She didn't even *risk* a look in the mirror! Talk about windswept!

At her farewell party at her old hospital last week Mick, one of the newly qualified doctors, had offered to drive her to Southbury on the back of his Harley-Davidson and Sarah, never one to refuse a challenge, had gaily accepted. It had been fun—intensely exhilarating but extremely heavy on the hairstyle—and she wasn't sure if she had left her stomach behind somewhere on the motorway!

Eager to settle herself in, she had sent Mick off home with a quick peck on the cheek and had promised to invite him to any nurses' parties at her new hospital.

Sarah glanced around the room quickly. It *was* small, she thought ruefully. But then she had been spoiled in the past, hadn't she? This was the first nurses' home she had ever stayed in. She had lived at home all the time during her nursing and then her midwifery training. And home was a palatial country pile with horses and stables and a swimming pool. A bit different to the cramped living space which was to be her home at Southbury Hospital.

Not for the first time she wondered if she had done the right thing to fly the nest and come here— to a hospital with a fine reputation, admittedly, but one where she knew absolutely *no one*!

But Sarah was by nature an optimist and she drew her shoulders back and strolled over to the window to see if the view was all it was cracked up to be.

And it was.

Stretching in front of her eyes for what seemed like miles, the city lay spread out before her. Like a sombre artist's palette, the neat rooftops of the city were coloured in myriad greys and browns. And rising up from the symmetry to meet the cloudless blue of the sky was the most perfect architectural structure of all—Southbury Cathedral dominated the entire landscape with its beauty and elegance.

'Wow!' exclaimed Sarah happily, as she turned to smile at the nurse who had been standing and watching her. 'You were certainly right about the view—it's magnificent! What an amazing cathedral!'

She pushed back the heavy lock of dark hair

that threatened to flop over her eye and glanced around the room, as if a little unsure of what to do next. And she *was* unsure, too! She had only been qualified as a midwife for just over two weeks! But her insecurity was gone in a flash—one thing Sarah Jackson had never been short on was confidence!

'Do you want any help settling in?' asked the nurse rather uncertainly.

Sarah shook her head. 'No, thanks,' she answered decisively. 'I'll unpack later. I think I'll wander down to the maternity unit and have a nose around.'

The other nurse frowned in confusion. 'But you're not on duty until Monday, surely?'

'True!' agreed Sarah breezily. 'But on Monday morning I'll be thrown in at the deep end. What if it's hellishly busy and a midwife or a doctor yells for something and I haven't got a clue where to find it?'

The nurse shrugged. 'They'd make allowances, of course.'

'But why should they *have* to make allowances?' queried Sarah reasonably. 'When, with a little effort on my part, I can know the layout of the department before I actually start?'

The nurse who, although kind-hearted, had a limited imagination looked as shocked as if Sarah had just proposed streaking onto the unit in a pair of roller-skates! 'But you aren't *authorised* to go to the unit,' she pointed out repressively, 'until Monday morning.'

'Rubbish!' answered Sarah cheerfully, mentally crossing this particular nurse off her list of would-be new friends.

'It's not rubbish!' replied the other girl a trifle heatedly. 'It's the rules!'

Sarah was the youngest of five children, spoilt rotten by her three sisters and beloved big brother, Benedict. And, much though they loved her, they would have been the first to point out that if Sarah had a fault it was that she tended to speak without thinking. Or, as Benedict always said, she engaged her foot before her mouth! 'Rules are made to be broken!' she declared rather passionately. 'It's Saturday morning—it shouldn't be *too* busy! And, besides, I can be very unobstrusive,' she fibbed outrageously. 'I'll just merge into the background.'

'I'll let you get on, then,' said the nurse blandly. Merge into the background indeed! Looking like *that*? Life had been very boring at Southbury recently. Nothing much had happened since the new paediatric staff nurse had fallen madly in love with the elusive Dr Le Saux.

But things were looking up! The nurse almost rubbed her hands together in glee as she anticipated the fireworks in the maternity unit with the arrival of this outspoken new midwife!

Jamie gently removed his fingertips from the patient's brachial pulse and stared down at her assessingly. She was exhausted—that much was clear. It was evident from her extreme pallor, the darkened smudges beneath her eyes and the way that her hair lay in limp, damp tendrils across her clammy brow.

He had seen her in his outpatients' clinic just a few days earlier—a fit and healthy thirty-year-old who had been one of those lucky women who had seemed to sail through her pregnancy, taking it completely in her stride.

She was not so lucky now, he thought.

Mrs Markham opened her eyes and gave him a weak smile. 'So, what's the verdict, Doc?'

He admired the attempted joke but correctly read the terrible fear in the woman's eyes. He never forgot that labour and childbirth were a mystery, often a terrifying one, to women who had never experienced it before.

He was also a doctor who never hid behind jargon or obscured the truth through well-meaning 'kindness'. And Mrs Markham was an intelligent woman. Ignoring the half-disapproving look from the ward sister, he sat down on the edge of the bed.

'Your labour isn't proceeding as well as we would have hoped,' he said slowly. 'You have been in labour for almost twenty-four hours and as this is your first baby—'

'You mean that as I'm a primigravida?' corrected the patient crisply, and Jamie smiled.

'Yes, I do. In a woman with a second or subsequent pregancy I would be reluctant to allow the labour to proceed past twelve hours. You've been given longer because first-time mums can be notoriously slow. However,' he paused, speaking carefully so that his words would be understood, 'your uterus is not contracting forcibly and rhythmically. The contractions are weak, irregular and intermittent. And although you are not unduly distressed by them you're getting pretty tired.

'I think you have a condition known as hypotonic inertia, probably, I suspect, because you have a large baby. But don't look so alarmed. The fancy Latin name just means that there is a delay in your labour. There is no immediate threat to either you or your baby. What we will do is introduce a commonly used drug into your bloodstream. We're going to try an oxytoxin infusion in an attempt to maintain regular contractions—'

Mrs Markham opened her eyes very wide. 'And will that work?'

Some patients deliberately avoided asking questions as though if they acknowledged risk then the worst might happen. This woman was most emphatically *not* one of those. Jamie's dazzling blue eyes were partially hidden by the outrageously thick lashes that framed them but he was totally oblivious to the impact that his looks had on women. Widowers had no time for vanity!

'It may work,' he told her honestly. 'It isn't always successful because although contractions occur they do not always succeed in dilating the cervix.'

'And then what?'

'Then a Caesarian section is necessary,' said Jamie and, seeing the look of disappointment that had crumpled her features, gave her hand a comforting squeeze, his eyes questioning. In his experience it was always best to let patients voice their fears about any invasive procedure.

Mrs Markham shook her head, biting her lips to hold back the tears. 'It doesn't seem fair,' she told him distractedly.

'What doesn't?'

She shook her head from side to side so that the damp, limp tendrils swayed around her white face. 'You think it's all going to be so easy! You go to all the childbirth classes and you do your breathing and your exercises religiously. They tell you how to avoid the use of drugs; how to have a baby the *natural* way. And now this.' Her voice trembled with emotion.

'I've already been sucking in gas and air like it was going out of fashion! I've been extremely tempted to have an injection of pethidine and now you're going to infuse me with some kind of drug to speed up my contractions. And if *that* doesn't work I'll be bundled off down to Theatre to have my belly sliced open!'

Jamie heard Sister suck in a disapproving breath behind him as she listened to the patient's rather florid description. Sister was of the old school— an excellent yet formidable midwife whose experience and confidence could calm down the most frightened of patients—but one, nevertheless, who believed that patients should just lie back and accept what the doctor or midwife told them without demur!

He smiled. 'You paint a vivid and graphic picture of the Caesarean,' he commented drily. 'And while, like all surgical procedures, it carries with it an element of risk—'

'Oh, it isn't just *that*!' blurted out Mrs Markham. 'Fear comes into it, yes, but it's just that I'm feeling so out of control!'

'I know,' said Jamie gently. 'Believe me, I know. A great number of women experience this feeling during childbirth. I'm a man—I can't even pretend to understand what it must be like but you must try not to be frightened. I *can* understand your frustration, particularly when you've worked so hard at your classes. But nature is a formidable force and it's easy to forget that. Sometimes babies just don't come the way we wanted them to and there's no shame attached to that. Natural birth may be preferable but it isn't always viable.

'The important thing is to deliver a healthy baby to a mother who isn't too exhausted to care for him or her.' He gave her hand another squeeze and stood up, pleased to see that the tight, anxious look had left her face.

'Are you happier with that?' he quizzed.

'Much happier,' said Mrs Markham with quiet fervency.

Jamie nodded his dark head. 'And just where is that husband of yours? I thought he wanted to be in on the birth.'

'Oh, but he does! His firm sent him to Paris on business—he should be landing at Heathrow any minute now.'

'Good. You'll feel even better when he's here to hold your hand.'

'Thank you, Doctor!'

He turned towards Sister. 'Could you organise for the infusion to be set up, please, Sister?'

Sister Singleton nodded her head and the out-dated and frilly cap, which she refused to abandon, bobbed up and down in a froth of lace as she did so. 'I'll go and check it with one of the pupil midwives now.'

'Where's Dr Alcott?' asked Jamie, as they moved towards the door. There had been no sign of the registrar since he had arrived. And consider-ing that he had been the one to call Jamie in because he wasn't happy about the way Mrs Markham was progressing it was peculiar behaviour for him not to be here, to say the least.

As he asked the question Sister shot him an odd look which, even to the least discerning person, would have had an underlying message. To Jamie the look spoke volumes.

'I'm glad you mentioned that, Jamie,' said Sister quietly, looking from side to side as though they might be overheard. 'I'd like to talk to you about Dr Alcott.'

'When?'

'Now, if you don't mind. I'll just go and organ-ise the drip then I'll come back along to my office and meet you there. I'll bring coffee, if you like— you look as though you could do with a cup. You were up most of the night delivering, so the night staff tell me.'

Jamie stifled his objection to hanging around the labour ward more than was absolutely necessary.

Clearly it *was* necessary and Sister obviously wanted to speak to him privately. She wasn't usually the kind of chatty ward sister who spent her time drinking coffee with the doctors. He also had that time-worn and usually fairly accurate gut feeling that he was going to be in Labour Ward for some time.

Deliberately refusing to allow himself to think about Harriet at the swimming pool, he dug his hands deep in the pockets of his trousers and walked along the corridor towards Sister's office, his mind busy composing a reply to a letter he had received from an American university that morning offering him a job. If it hadn't been for Harriet and the prospect of unsettling her he might have been tempted to accept. Very tempted.

At the other end of the corridor a figure halted and froze.

Sarah stood and stared at the authoritative-looking man who was walking slowly towards her, his hands slung in his trouser pockets, obviously miles away.

Who the hell was *he*?

Trapped in the sensual claws of her first experience of instant and overwhelming attraction, Sarah stood stock-still in the middle of the corridor as she watched the man approach. She felt her heart clenching with some kind of primitive recognition, as though an alien hand had reached through her chest wall and squeezed it very tightly. She forgot to breathe. Her pulse rocketed. She almost sagged back against the wall in fright.

Fright? Who did she think she was kidding?

As she watched the man grow closer she felt flooded with the most extraordinary sense of elation. Could there be such a thing as love at first sight? she wondered wildly. She didn't stop to think what she must look like and even if she had she would not have cared. She was being carried along on the strength of some emotion that she had never experienced in her life before. She had to talk to him. She simply *had* to!

'Hello!' she said boldly and stood directly in his path, giving him the benefit of her biggest, brightest smile. Sarah's brother had always said that her smile could have charmed the birds off the trees. She had never even been conscious of its charm before but now she was. She wanted to charm this man more than she had ever wanted anything in her life.

Jamie frowned, suddenly and unaccountably wary, as his eyes swept assessingly over the young woman who was blocking his path. She oozed confidence, he thought. Simply oozed it. A confidence which was usually only found in stunningly beautiful women, in his experience. And this woman was no beauty.

Not classically, anyway.

And then he looked a little more closely and frowned again.

Not beautiful, no. But something else. Something. . . He tried to analyse it.

She was fairly tall and she carried herself superbly, with poise and stature. As though someone had taught her from an early age to always walk as though there were two heavy books on top of that thick, shiny dark hair.

And her limbs were superbly proportioned; muscular but with the kind of natural strength that came from playing sport—not the kind of artificial muscle tone that resulted from hours and hours spent in the gym. The healthy curves of hip and breast were slender, yet full. Someone who looked as though she enjoyed her food without being ruled by it. Not a woman obsessed with magazine images, striving for an unnatural pre-pubescent shape, for whom food had become her body's enemy. She had the body of a woman. Botticelli would have approved, Jamie thought ruefully. Almost as much as he did.

And she had the bright sparkle of youth and energy, too—her cheeks pink and glowing and her eyes alive and dancing. And what eyes! They were green and clever and slanting—the most astonishing shade of emerald that he could ever remember seeing. But then he creased his forehead so that his dark brows almost met as a distant bell of memory jangled in the depths of his mind but her physical presence was so arresting that the fleeting memory was consigned to oblivion.

She wore the thin, pale blue cotton, short-sleeved top and trousers and clogs that only the theatre staff normally wore and yet he could have sworn that she didn't work here. He would have recognised her instantly if he had seen her before.

Something about her stole into him like the

warmth of the first spring day after a hard, unforgiving winter and Jamie stiffened defensively.

It was like having a fantasy come to life and Sarah was *dying* to hear him speak. 'Hello,' she said again, more softly this time, but the smile remained undiminished in its brilliance.

Jamie saw danger in that smile—a danger that he didn't dare attempt to define. Biting back the urge to respond to her greeting as eagerly as a cat would lap at a bowlful of cream, he tightened his mouth instead. 'Who are you?' he demanded, his deep voice roughened and harsh. 'Do you work here?'

Her fantasy daydream dissolved into dust. She swallowed back the disappointment. 'I don't actually work here—' she replied. She had been about to add, 'not yet,' when she saw his rather sensational mouth twist from that horrible hard line into a curve of critical censure.

Jamie was so disorientated by a curious and potent cocktail of desire, coupled with intense irritation, that he was scarcely aware of what he was saying. 'Then what the hell are you doing here?' His glare increased.

Hospitals were no longer the safe havens of days gone by. A few devastating incidents of kidnapping from various maternity units in different parts of the country over the past few years had heightened public awareness of the need to protect hospitals from the whims of disturbed strangers.

Sarah was unused to such blatant hostility. It felt like diving headlong into uncharted and unpleasant waters. She bristled with indignation. 'What on earth do you *think* I'm doing here?' she demanded, trying not to think about what a fabulous pair of blue eyes he had.

Jamie shrugged and the subtle interplay of muscles didn't escape Sarah's notice! She felt her heart renew its quickened pace even while she glared back at him.

'How should I know?' he responded dismissively, common sense returning as he concentrated fiercely on blotting out the very physical impact she was having on him. 'You aren't wearing a name-badge. Are you? You could be anyone.' He saw her dark brows rise in disbelief and he nodded slowly. 'Yes,' he affirmed. '*Anyone*. You could be on your way to kidnap one of the babies in the postnatal ward, for all I know.'

Sarah wavered between exploding with rage and exploding with laughter and laughter won. He was much too gorgeous to shout at! Her green eyes crinkled at the corners in a disturbingly familiar way to Jamie. She held her hands up in appeal, palms facing out. 'Do I really *look* like a kidnapper?' she appealed in a throaty murmur.

Jamie realised that he was being absurd but he couldn't stop himself. If he disapproved of her it helped. Helped him, that was. If the disapproval went then that might mean that he would do something completely out of character and kiss those full, sweet lips until she begged him to take her.

Appalled at the rampant line his thoughts had taken, he forced himself to behave reasonably. 'I have no idea.' His voice was cool. 'Fortunately, I have never been acquainted with a kidnapper.' How preposterous this conversation would sound to an outsider, he thought with a disturbing flash of insight.

'I'm sure you haven't,' agreed Sarah, deadpan.

She was laughing at him! Damn the woman, thought Jamie angrily, and then realised something else, too. That he was becoming unbearably aroused. Dear Lord, how pathetic could he get? Turned on by a foxy-eyed stranger just because she had had the gall to confront him?

He sucked air into his lungs. He scrabbled around for some of his customary authority, remembering the calm, assured way that he had spoken to Mrs Markham just a few minutes ago. He duplicated that voice now with the eagerness with which a drowning man would have clutched onto a raft.

'I dare say that you have a perfectly bona fide reason for wandering around the unit without a name-badge,' he observed coolly, 'although I note that you still have not provided me with a satisfactory explanation.'

Sarah's good humour was evaporating very quickly. Disappointed that her supposed knight in shining armour was turning out to have the disposition of a high court judge with dyspepsia was bad enough but to have him talk to her in that—that *patronising* way of his. Well! She lifted her chin in what only her family and closest friends would have recognised as the first sign of one of 'Sarah's paddies'.

'And why the hell should I provide *you* with a ''satisfactory explanation''?' she mimicked angrily.

Jamie did something that he had never done before, not in all his years as a doctor.

He pulled rank.

'Because I'm the consultant in charge of the unit?' he suggested arrogantly, outraged by her unblinking look of boredom.

Sarah wasn't in the least bit fazed by his statement. Her father was a retired professor of surgery and her big brother was a consultant at one of London's largest teaching hospitals. What did he expect her to do—start genuflecting at his feet? 'So?' she responded coolly.

Jamie was floored by her attitude. He had been working at Southbury Hospital for just under a year and in that time he had never had a cross word with another person. He found himself wondering briefly what it would be like to subdue this beautiful, spirited creature and then realised too late that such thoughts were taking him irresistibly up the path of desire again.

Determined to win something warmer from her than the frosty look of disapproval that she was currently subjecting him to, Jamie gave her the smile that he normally reserved for his favourite patients and tried reason again. 'I'm sure that if you were a mother who had just given birth,' he began, using the same voice that had given Mrs

Markham such reassurance earlier, 'then you would not rest easy if you thought that unidentified people were being allowed to walk around the unit unchallenged.'

He *did* have a point, Sarah acknowledged reluctantly, and she gladly let her disapproval slip away.

'Would you?' he persisted, noting with pleasure the way that her eyes had begun to glow with green fire again.

'No,' she admitted, with a grin. 'Shall we start again?' she added disarmingly and held one long, slender-fingered hand out towards him. 'Sarah Jackson,' she said. 'Fully qualified midwife—as of two weeks ago!'

Her name had stirred some faint, long-suppressed memory but Jamie was so caught up with the desire to touch her that he paid it no heed. He extended his own hand, caught the cool, silky-satin smoothness of hers and resisted the urge to run his fingers lingeringly up and down the skin. 'Jamie Brennan,' he smiled. 'And I think I've already stated my reason for being here. Overstated it, in fact,' he added in a self-deprecating aside.

Sarah gave another sunny smile, not noticing that her hand was still locked tightly in his warm grasp. 'Oh, that's OK,' she said breezily. 'You *were* quite right to challenge me.'

'So do you—work here?' he queried, his breath unconsciously catching in his throat as his body acknowledged how important her answer was to him, even if his mind was not so easy to convince.

'I start on Monday,' said Sarah happily, as she observed that his sensational mouth had softened slightly and that the thick, black fringe of his lashes wasn't managing to conceal the sapphire brilliance of his eyes.

Jamie seemed to be caught in a sensual time warp. Instinctively he let the pad of one thumb slide slowly across the soft palm of her hand and Sarah almost fainted with the shock of how much pleasure such a seemingly innocent gesture could produce. She often wondered afterwards what would have happened next had not a sound interrupted them.

'Jamie!' came a voice and Sister Singleton came hurrying down the corridor towards them and one look at her astonished face reminded Jamie that he was still holding Sarah's hand. To let it fall would have seemed a kind of betrayal and he squeezed it before breaking contact. But, compared to the comforting squeeze he often gave to patients, this one felt positively X-rated!

'Hello, Sister,' he said calmly.

'Jamie,' nodded Sister pleasantly, turning her attention to the young woman beside him.

Sarah, who was just discovering what blushing felt like for the first time in her life, read the question in the senior nurse's eyes.

'Hello, Sister,' she said, rather breathlessly. 'I'm Sarah Jackson. One of your new midwives.'

'Sarah Jackson?' frowned Sister.

'That's right! I'm not really supposed to start until Monday but I thought. . .thought. . .' she gave a beseeching smile '. . .that I'd have a look around the department to sort of familiarise myself with things. Just in case I didn't know where to look for things on Monday,' she finished lamely.

Sister Singleton nodded her greying hair, amused to note that the tension between the two young people was—as the best books always put it—charged! So Jamie Brennan was getting interested in women at last, was he? And not before time, either! But her face remained bland as she said, 'That was very commendable of you, Staff Nurse. Have you seen everything you want to see?' she queried politely although, judging by the girl's face, the question was purely academic!

Sarah remained transfixed by jewel-bright eyes and the memory of that lingering, stroking movement of his thumb that had rather indecently suggested things to her which she was only just discovering existed! 'Oh, yes, um—thanks, Sister!' she said.

Jamie, still caught up in the spell that she had woven around him, was unwilling to see her go lest he discover that he had just dreamt her up and was just working out how he could keep her waiting until Sister had said whatever it was that she wanted to say to him when there was a kerfuffle at the door.

The three of them looked up to see a tall, slim man with blond curly hair, dressed entirely in squashy black leathers and with an expensive pair of sunglasses obscuring his eyes. He looked mean and sexy and very slightly dangerous. Underneath his arm he carried a helmet, although a guitar wouldn't have looked out of place since he resembled the lead singer of an extremely well-known rock band!

What the hell is Mick still doing here? thought Sarah with a sinking heart. Just when she was sure that she was winning Sister over, too. And although Mick might be the prize-winning doctor of his generation—the one-to-watch, as all the consultants were currently saying—why, oh, why did he have to strut around the place looking as though he was about to start a revolution?

'Hi, babe!' said Mick cheerfully. 'They told me I'd find you here.'

Jamie swallowed down distaste, jealousy and the violent desire to punch this no-good layabout in the teeth!

But Sister Singleton was not too old to recognise outrageous sex appeal even if the possessor of it did look like a rock star. She put on her sternest voice but for once it did not sound in the least bit convincing. 'Would you mind telling me what you're doing in this department, young man?'

Mick took his sunglasses off and Sister was nearly rocked off her feet by the impact of golden brown eyes and a brilliant white smile set in the kind of face that could only be described as pure perfection. 'Sure can, Sister,' he said, in his deep, distinctive drawl. 'I came looking for Sarah—and now I've found her.'

The look of disgust on Jamie Brennan's face making her feel sick, Sarah decided that there was nothing to do but go. And go quickly.

'Thank you for letting me look around, Sister,' she said hastily. 'And I look forward to seeing you on Monday. Goodbye, Mr Brennan,' she ventured tentatively. 'It was nice to have met you.'

But Jamie didn't answer.

CHAPTER TWO

SISTER Singleton looked at her consultant, who sat on the other side of her desk, and took a deep breath before launching forth.

'The thing is, Jamie, it's not that I don't *like* the man—I do. Or, rather, I *think* I do! And I think he's a very good doctor, too; he just isn't giving any of us a chance. He's become distant and that's in a few short weeks. From being the kind of man I would trust to deliver my niece's baby he's become the kind of man I wouldn't let near my pet dog—and she's delivered four sets of puppies on her own very nicely, thank you!

'Jamie?' Sister Singleton's white cap wobbled like an uncooked meringue as she leaned forward and prompted, '*Jamie*?'

Jamie glanced up and blinked. 'Hmm?'

'Have you heard a single word I've said to you?'

Jamie lifted his broad shoulders in appeal, then shook his dark head. 'Actually, no. I haven't. Sorry, Sister.' He had been too busy torturing himself with visions of just what kind of activities Sarah Jackson and her motorbiking Adonis were currently engaging in. Unfortunately every one of the visions involved both participants in various stages of undress and Jamie had repeatedly kicked the leg of his chair, very hard, without even realising that he was doing so.

Sister smiled with genuine pleasure. She had worked with Jamie Brennan for almost a year and he was the best doctor that she had ever encountered. He had never, in all that time, set a foot wrong or done a thing that would have invited idle gossip about him. How encouraging, then, to see that he could be human after all!

'I was talking to you about Dr Alcott,' she reminded him softly.

Jamie forced himself back to the present with an effort and concentrated on his new registrar. 'What's wrong with him?'

'I don't know. But I'm not happy with him.'

Jamie nodded. Nor was he. Alcott seemed to have lost every bit of confidence he had possessed in the few short weeks he had been at Southbury. Which would account for why he had been calling his consultant in to assist him with things that, by rights, a registrar should have easily been able to deal with himself—even a fairly inexperienced one.

Jamie sighed. What with Harriet's increasingly dissatisfied behaviour and the headache of having to find himself a new nanny this was one problem he did *not* need.

'It must be a burden on you, too,' said Sister perceptively. 'I haven't seen you look this tired before.'

'Oh, I'm OK,' said Jamie automatically. 'It would help if Ellen wasn't away on holiday but she is and that's all there is to it.' He missed the assistance of his senior registrar, who was hard-working, fun and extremely bright.

'Beats me how she can afford to go to Bali on a doctor's salary,' said Sister rather jealously.

'She's married to a pilot,' said Jamie with a wink and then stood up. 'I'll have a think about Dr Alcott. Maybe take him out for a couple of drinks and see if I can find out what's worrying him.'

Sister nodded. 'That would be great.'

Jamie glanced at his watch. 'I'm due to take my daughter swimming,' he said. 'Let me know how Mrs Markham goes. I'm on the long-range bleeper if you think she looks as though we might need to take her to Theatre. I'll just pop my head round the door of the special care baby unit and have a quick look at last night's prem baby before I go.'

'Right,' said Sister briskly, and glanced up. 'Have a good swim!'

Back in her room Sarah was trembling, causing Mick to look at her with some concern.

'Are you all right, babe?' he queried solici-tously.

Sarah had never particularly minded Mick call-ing her 'babe' before; she had never really given it a thought, to be honest. After all, he was just one of a large group of people she had knocked around with at her training hospital. But now she felt like shouting at him to stop and it wouldn't take a genius to work out why. Just when Jamie

Brennan had calmed down and curbed his grumpiness—even to the extent of holding her hand for much longer than was necessary—Mick had appeared and the atmosphere had changed from sunshine to Siberia in a couple of seconds.

'Of course I'm all right,' she said crossly. 'I just wasn't expecting to see you, that's all.'

'You made *that* pretty obvious,' said Mick rather drily. 'But I went outside to discover that the big end had gone on my bike and the garage may not be able to get hold of the part until tomorrow. Mind if I stay the night, Sarah?'

Sarah gave him a look of sheer horror. *Now* what had she got herself into? She had agreed to his offer of a lift, yes, but surely that didn't mean that he expected. . .expected. . . 'But there's only one bed!' she declared shrilly.

Mick threw back his head and laughed and laughed. 'Oh, Sarah,' he said eventually, wiping his eyes at the corners. 'You're such an innocent, aren't you?'

Sarah glared at him. Right at this moment she didn't want to *be* an innocent. Right at this moment she wanted to be so pouting and *dripping* with blatant invitation and sex appeal that Jamie Brennan would come dashing to the nurses' home and kick the door in and throw her on the bed and. . .and. . .

'Sarah, why are you blushing?' asked Mick curiously.

Twice in one day! How on earth could you spend twenty-five years of your life without blushing and then do it twice in one day? Sarah asked herself despairingly.

'I don't want to sleep with you, you ninny,' Mick told her gently.

Sarah sighed. It was almost funny. Mick had entirely misconstrued the reason for the two livid flares of colour, she decided after a reluctant glance in the mirror.

Mick put his helmet down on the coffee-table and gave her an appealing look. 'I'll crash on your floor, if need be.'

'Yes, OK, OK,' said Sarah distractedly, wishing that he would stop going on about it. She needed to get away. On her own. To think. Or would she just brood? Gratefully she remembered the membership to the country club which her father had given her as a going-away present. 'I'm going out for a while to get some fresh air,' she told Mick and then, as she saw the hopeful glint in his eyes, added firmly, 'On my *own*! You don't mind, do you, Mick?'

Mick shook his abundant blond curls and grinned. 'Not at all. I'll just have a mosey around the place—apparently there are the most *amazing* brass rubbings in Southbury Cathedral. I'll catch you later. Buy you a beer and a curry, if you like.'

Sarah watched him go with some bemusement. Brass rubbings? He really was the most surprising man!

She glanced around the room. She hadn't even unpacked her suitcase yet but so what? There was no mother to nag her about tidying her room any more! And, besides, she felt really rather restless. And the room felt stiflingly claustrophobic. Her father had told her that the country club was rather plush, with fantastic facilities. A bit of hard physical exercise would do her no end of good.

Bending down, she scrabbled around in her suitcase until she had extracted a lime-green bikini.

'So, did the lady have her baby, Daddy?' Panting from doing three fast lengths in the Olympic-sized outdoor pool, Harriet flopped down dripping wet onto one of the towels which Marianne had spread out in the sunshine.

'Not yet, darling.' Jamie eyed the water with a little shudder, mentally gearing himself up to dive into the cool, blue depths.

'Why not?'

'The baby was being slow. So we gave the lady a drug to see if that would help the baby come quicker.'

'I thought drugs were bad news?' said Harriet, unconsciously reciting the words of the community policeman who had arrived at her school recently to give a lecture on the evils of legal and illegal substances.

'Not the ones that Daddy prescribes,' explained Jamie patiently, flexing his muscles in anticipation. He shot a sideways glance at Marianne whose straight up-and-down figure made a mockery of the amount of food she put away. 'Ready for that race now, Marianne?' he challenged.

But Marianne's eyes were fixed on the opposite

side of the pool. Jamie followed her gaze and saw a group of her school friends, drinking cans of soft drinks and laughing in the loud and affected way common to teenagers the world over. 'Think I'll go and have a chat with my mates instead,' she said. 'Now that you're here to keep an eye on Harriet. If that's OK?'

Jamie nodded. How absolutely typical! Now he was even being deprived of the chance of showing off in front of his nanny! Of putting her to shame for having the temerity to refer to him as middle-aged!

'Can I have an ice-cream, Daddy?' piped up Harriet.

'Yes, all right. Take some money from my wallet. And sit in the shade while you eat it,' he said automatically. 'Otherwise you'll burn up. Oh, and Harriet—I'm going for a swim so don't get back in the water unless you tell me first.'

'Yes, Daddy.' Harriet screwed up her freckle-spattered nose. 'There's no need to nag!'

Jamie blew her a don't-be-cheeky kiss and dived into the water cleanly then struck out, marvelling at how swimming was like cycling—something you never forgot!

But an image of Sarah swam into his mind and he closed his eyes as he felt the full throb of desire make itself felt. Damn and damn and damn! What was it with him? With her? That he should suddenly start behaving like a randy young adolescent after years of relatively trouble-free celibacy?

He moved his arms in increasingly powerful

arcs, trying to exhaust himself and reminding himself over and over again just how cool the water was in an attempt to damp down his ardour. Otherwise, he thought in dismay, he would be stuck in the pool until the last person had gone home!

In one of the wooden-doored changing-rooms Sarah clambered into her lime-green bikini, groaning softly to herself as she hoicked the bottom up. She had put on weight! Though that was hardly surprising. She bent her head to one side to survey the generous curve of her hip and pulled a face.

She knew what must have been responsible. There had been almost an entire week of 'goodbye' parties at her old hospital. She shuddered to think how many glasses of white wine and wedges of cake she must have eaten! And now she was paying the price!

The narrow waistband was digging in painfully and her lush breasts were barely decent, not really contained at all by the two tiny triangles of green Lycra which comprised the top.

Oh, well. She wasn't planning to parade around the side of the pool like some *Baywatch* babe! She was here for a swim and a spot of discreet sunbathing. And she should be quite safe—this was hardly the most lively place on earth! She pushed the door of the cubicle open and looked around. There were a few middle-aged couples, a group of teenagers and just one man in the water who was swimming with all the determination of someone doing Olympic trials. With a bit of luck he would soon get out and she could have the entire pool to herself!

She slung her striped canvas holdall over one shoulder and was beginning to pick her way across the grass when she had to swerve to avoid being cannoned into by a child of about nine who was so intent on licking her ice-lolly that she wasn't looking where she was going.

'Whoops!' said Sarah, rapidly removing herself from the path of the lolly and automatically putting a hand out in case the child stumbled. 'Steady!'

The child looked up. Pretty little thing, thought Sarah immediately, with those unusual amber eyes and strawberry-blonde hair. The style was a bit old-fashioned, though. Fancy having it tied in those thick braids! It made her look not unlike Heidi.

Sarah smiled and the child relaxed a little but Sarah was acutely aware that these days most children were taught never to talk to strangers but as she made to move on the child said, 'The ice-cream man will be leaving in half an hour. If you want to buy one.'

'Thanks,' Sarah gravely. 'I'll remember that.' She frowned. The ice that the child was eating looked like an imploding spinach on the end of a stick. 'Is that nice?' she asked doubtfully.

'Lovely! Want a lick?' challenged the child, with the assurance of one who knew that her request would be refused.

'No, thanks.' Sarah shook her dark head.

The child put her head to one side. 'Why doesn't your bikini fit properly?'

Sarah pulled an expressive face. Out of the mouths of babes! 'Oh, I ate too much and got fat,' she said ruefully.

'My mummy got thin,' said the child mournfully, her features suddenly sharpening and making her appear years older. Then she turned abruptly and walked off.

Sarah blinked as she watched her. Strange. The way the little girl had looked just then. It was not a look that she had seen before and Sarah was good with children. Which was not really surprising. She had loads of nephews and nieces and recently she had been made godmother to her brother Benedict's new baby.

Verity, Benedict's wife, had produced a bouncing baby boy just four months ago. But it had not been an easy birth. In fact, it had been touch and go for a while—for both mother and baby—and Verity had had to stay in hospital for almost a fortnight with Benedict camping in his wife's room, terrified that if he left her side he would lose her.

Sarah had been given the job of looking after their older daughter, Sammi; of keeping her amused and allaying her fears. The two of them had got along famously. She couldn't be very much younger than the little girl with the braided hair and the sad face, thought Sarah, watching as the child walked over to a giant oak tree and sat down beneath it in the shade. There was no sign of her mother, either.

She put her stuff down on the grass and put the child out of her mind. It was none of her business, after all. Looking down at the ground to spot any stray pieces of sharp stone, Sarah carefully picked her way over the grass towards the pool.

Jamie, doing a leisurely breast-stroke, had always been extremely sceptical about the phenomenon known as a mirage but for a moment he thought that he had just magicked up his own private optical illusion. He blinked his eyes. Sarah Jackson was standing on the edge of the pool, wearing a ridiculously small bikini which was doing dangerous things to his blood pressure. And he forgot all the vows he had made in Sister's office—about not getting involved with someone whom he sensed could bring danger into his life. He even forgot the insane jealousy he had felt towards the biker who had come to find her.

Jamie scanned the pool and its surrounding area but there was no sign of any accompanying man.

And suddenly nothing mattered other than the urge to dampen his ardour before he confronted her. He dropped down to the bottom of the pool then surfaced again.

She was no longer there.

The unbearable sense of disappointment he experienced lasted only for as long as it took for him to realise that she had simply dived into the water and was, at that moment, making her way towards the far end of the pool in a determined crawl.

For the second time that day Jamie felt like a teenager. He dived right to the bottom and then swam the whole length underneath the water as fast as he had ever swum in his life. He saw the shadowy curves of two shapely legs above him and, after a last spurt of power, he surfaced directly in front of her, ridiculously pleased at the look of shocked pleasure he saw on her face.

'*You*!' she exclaimed. Sarah recognised him immediately and saw no point in pretending otherwise; she was much too straightforward and sexually naïve to play the game of feigning ignorance.

Her lips opened to form an unconsciously provocative pout and Jamie felt literally weak with longing. What would she do if he kissed her? he wondered hungrily. With a monumental effort he pushed the thought away.

'Yes, me,' he agreed, treading water. 'What are you doing here?'

Her eyes teased him for asking the obvious and Sarah discovered for the first time in her life that it could be fun to flirt. 'The same as you,' she dimpled.

He hoped not. He hoped that she wasn't experiencing the same overwhelming desire as he—to peel that outrageous costume from her lush, young body and to lose himself in it. . .

Sarah looked into his eyes, which were as blue as the sky on a holiday postcard, and read something there that was way beyond her experience as a woman but not beyond her comprehension. Perhaps she should have felt anger or indignation at his expression of desire and yet she could not find it in herself to feel anything other than flattered. . .

'That wasn't what I meant,' he said, fascinated by the droplets of water that ran in such enticing rivulets down her lightly tanned skin, disappearing into the deep cleft between her breasts.

'Oh?' Sarah raised her brows, her bright green eyes silently laughing. 'And just what *did* you mean?'

He forced himself to concentrate on the mundane for she would have a fit if he said what he really wanted to say. . . 'Just that we don't have many nurses as members here,' he observed. 'None, in fact.' God! How middle-aged that made him sound! Maybe Marianne had been right.

Sarah bristled. She had been a nurse for long enough to be acutely and often painfully aware that, compared to doctors at least, nurses were second-rate citizens. 'Meaning that nurses lower the tone of the place, I suppose?' she demanded with a glower.

'That wasn't what I meant at all,' he said softly. 'But the annual subscription would be a big chunk out of wages which continue to be infuriatingly low.' He shot her a questioning look.

'You mean you were wondering how on earth I could afford to be here among the hallowed ranks of physicians?' Sarah demanded archly.

His eyes flickered with amusement at her defensiveness. 'Forgive me,' he murmured. 'I was prying.'

She met his gaze defiantly, overcome with an inexplicable urge to try to shock him. 'I have an extremely generous sugar-daddy,' she purred sultrily. 'And he gives me anything I want.'

His amusement vanished and, for a moment, Jamie was speechless. Horrified, outraged and speechless until he saw the humour which made her slanting eyes dance with green stars and he realised that she was teasing him. He experienced a renewed tide of longing. And so he teased her back. It was that or kiss her.

'Might I then suggest,' he drawled throatily, 'that you get him to invest in a new costume for you?' His eyes flicked lazily to the lush swell of her breasts which were spilling out of the frivolous green top she wore, their tips quite clearly outlined by a mixture of cool water and the prickling excitement of sexual awareness. 'You seem to have outgrown the one you're wearing!'

Sarah followed the direction of his eyes. Heavens! She looked positively indecent. Her cheeks flared up and she did the only thing possible in the circumstances—she dived beneath the surface of the water and swam away from him for all she was worth.

Jamie let her go, suppressing the urge to chase her—to flick water over her and splash her. To hoist her atop his shoulders and wade through the pool with those strong thighs locked around him. . . Those grown-up water frolics were just subliminal sex games—a socially acceptable way in which two partially clothed adults could touch one another in public.

And Jamie had been too long without any kind of sensual release to trust himself larking about in the water with someone as lovely as Sarah. Besides which his daughter was here.

Oh, Lord! In the heat of the moment he had forgotten all about Harriet. And this day out was supposed to be for *her* benefit. Guiltily Jamie hauled himself out of the water and, dripping wet, made his way across the grass towards Harriet, where she sat watching him, stony-faced.

'Hi!' he called with a grin, but she pretended not to have heard him and he could see a distinctly disapproving look on her face as he approached.

'Who was that girl?' she demanded.

'Girl?' For a moment he was genuinely confused until he realised who Harriet was talking about. The last way he would have described Sarah would have been as 'girl', he thought longingly. No, indeed, she was all woman.

'The fat one,' said Harriet tightly.

Jamie laughed until he recognised the nasty little snipe for what it was—jealousy; unfair but understandable. He drew in a deep breath, recognising that he would have to tread very carefully here. 'Her name is Sarah,' he told her, 'and she's one of the midwives at the hospital.'

'I've never seen her before,' said Harriet in a small, strained voice.

'No. That's because she's new. She doesn't officially start until Monday.'

'Oh.' Harriet looked from beneath her lashes to see her father following the progress of the woman who now cleaved her way through the water, doggedly swimming up and down as though her life depended on it. 'I love you, Daddy!' she said suddenly, and hurled herself into his arms for a hug.

'And I love you too, sweetheart,' said Jamie softly as he kissed the top of the strawberry-blonde hair. Guiltily he dragged his eyes away from the water. He needed to get away from here. And fast. 'We'd better call Marianne,' he said. 'And then maybe we could think about packing up a picnic—the Southbury Hills should be glorious on a day like today. What do you reckon?'

His daughter, surprisingly, made no objection to this, even though she had only been at the pool for just over an hour. And when Marianne arrived Harriet jumped up and hurled her arms around her as though she was some beloved and long-lost relative. Jamie was a little bemused by such an overt and unusual display of affection and it wasn't until he saw a pair of slanting green eyes observing them from the safety of the pool that he realised just who the show had been for.

CHAPTER THREE

THE receptionist looked from Sarah to Mick and back to Sarah again and said doubtfully, 'He looks all right to me.'

'No,' explained Sarah very patiently, thinking that just because Mick had the face of a fallen angel didn't mean that he was immune to injury! 'He definitely needs to see a doctor. I think he's fractured his wrist.'

The receptionist who sat behind the counter at Southbury's accident and emergency department gave Sarah a suspicious stare. 'How do you know what he's fractured?' she demanded. 'You a doctor or something?'

Sarah shook her head. 'No, I'm not. But I am a nurse. A midwife, as a matter of fact, and I work here.' The department was busy and Sarah was tired. Too tired to make the qualification that she did not actually start work until Monday.

'Oh, I see,' said the receptionist, slightly mollified. 'That's different, then.' She nodded her head towards the waiting-room which was full to bursting with injuries of varying degrees of seriousness. 'It's Saturday night,' she stated unnecessarily. 'You might have to wait a long time to see someone.'

'Ouch!' squealed Mick dramatically.

'Oh, do shut up, Mick,' Sarah told him unsympathetically. 'Moaning about it won't help.'

'You're a hard woman,' he complained half-
heartedly.

'Just go and sit down. I'll fill the form in for
you. He's just visiting,' Sarah explained to the
receptionist.

'You'll have to put *your* name and address
down, then,' said the other woman, 'if your
friend's just a temporary resident.'

Very temporary, Sarah hoped! 'OK,' she
responded brightly but she couldn't help pulling
an expressive face. The receptionist grinned.

'That sort of day, was it?' she queried, as she
handed Sarah the casualty form.

Sarah nodded. You could say that again! The
unthinkable had occurred. The man she fancied
like crazy was simply not available. Jamie Brennan
was married or, at least, that's what it had looked
like to an outsider. He had been in that cosy little
threesome—she had seen it with her very own
eyes. And no wonder the little girl had talked about
her mother getting thin. Thin wasn't in it—the
woman with Jamie looked as though a puff of wind
would blow her away. And, apart from anything
else, she looked so outrageously *young*.

Sarah bit her lip, oddly disappointed at Jamie
Brennan's behaviour. She was not sure what she
had expected of him but such obvious deception
had certainly not featured on her list!

She simply could not believe that he had flirted
quite so outrageously with *her*—with his wife and

daughter beside the pool! What kind of a man did that?

Which just goes to show what a pathetic innocent *you* are, Sarah Jackson, she told herself in disgust as she picked up the pen and began to fill in the accident and emergency form.

She had left the pool soon after Jamie had departed and had gone home in a stinking temper and had sat down in her new flat, surrounded by suitcases that she couldn't even be bothered to unpack.

So it had been a welcome diversion when Mick had arrived back from his trip round the city centre, virtually salivating over the brass rubbings he had been examining in Southbury Cathedral all afternoon. He had been in one of his best, wise-cracking moods and so Sarah had allowed him to talk her into going out for a drink and a curry, thinking that it might help rid her of her black mood.

And what a mistake *that* had been!

Usually, because he and his motorbike were virtually inseparable, Mick did not drink. But, tonight, unable to ride his motorbike home because of the missing part, he had decided to make the most of it. He had been swaying from an unaccustomed fourth pint of beer and by the time that Sarah had helped him out of the Southbury Tandoori House he had tripped over a wonky paving-stone and damaged his arm.

Men! thought Sarah darkly as Jamie Brennan's duplicity came to mind, vowing to ignore the two-timing lecherous creep from O and G the very next time she saw him.

She was handing over the completed casualty form to the receptionist when she heard someone shouting.

'Excuse me! Excuse me! Can somebody help me?' The shout was anxious and heartfelt.

Sarah glanced up to see that there was some sort of commotion at the door as a man appeared, half carrying a woman wearing only a nightdress who would have been doubled up in pain had not the advanced stage of her pregnancy prevented her from doing so.

'Quickly!' called the man unsteadily. 'Please! It's my wife—she's having a baby!'

'Not right now, I hope,' Sarah heard the receptionist mutter darkly as she reached for a button on her desk to ring for a nurse.

At that moment all hell broke loose. An ambulance siren was heard, getting louder and louder as it approached the A and E department, while at the same time a distinctive wailing sound began.

'Oh, shoot!' cursed the receptionist as the sound reverberated throughout the entire department. 'They've got a cardiac arrest in crash!' She looked around helplessly until she spotted a male nurse hurrying past. 'Is somebody dealing with that ambulance?' she demanded.

'Not me,' answered the nurse. 'I've been sent out to find the spare resuscitation trolley—we've got a huge bleed in cubicle four!'

'*Please*!' called the man accompanying the

pregnant woman, who had now slid moaning onto a chair hastily vacated by a man swigging from a bottle of cider. 'Can somebody *please* help my wife?'

Sarah looked anxiously over at the woman. She had only been qualified as a midwife for a few weeks and was very short on experience but even she could tell that the woman was in an advanced state of labour. She leaned over the desk to speak to the receptionist. 'Isn't anyone coming to attend to her?'

The receptionist shrugged. 'Search me. I've rung and no one's bothered answering.'

'We need to get her into the privacy of a cubicle, at least,' said Sarah. 'It can't be much fun having contractions with the world and his wife watching you.'

'It can't be much fun having contractions anyway!' quipped the receptionist, but Sarah did not smile.

'Can you find me a cubicle?' she demanded urgently. 'I can watch over her, if you like.'

The receptionist looked at her doubtfully. 'You aren't covered, though, are you?'

It was ironic how the caring professions had changed over the years, thought Sarah wryly. Her father, an eminent former surgeon himself, had often commented on it. These days the welfare of the patient became of secondary interest: the staff's number one priority seemed to be whether or not they could be sued for malpractice!

'No, I'm not covered! But I'm only planning to

sit with the woman until we can get her up to the labour ward!' Sarah snapped. 'I'm not intending to deliver her baby for her! So would you please tell me which cubicle we can take her to?'

The receptionist eyed Sarah's fierce look of determination and caved in. 'Number three,' she told her.

'Good,' said Sarah. 'Now I'd like you to emergency bleep the obstetrician on duty. Can you do that *now*?' The urgency and unusual nature of the situation she found herself in gave her voice an unaccustomed ring of authority.

'Can do,' said the receptionist and picked up the phone immediately.

'And what about me?' moaned Mick from a nearby chair, waving his damaged arm in the air for good effect and then wincing.

'You're in perfectly good hands!' retorted Sarah crisply. 'And you can wait. This lady can't.' She walked resolutely over to the pregnant woman who was weeping copiously and rocking backwards and forwards in pain, her husband bending over her with concern, his face a study in anxiety. Sarah touched the husband's arm and he straightened up immediately and stared at Sarah non-comprehendingly.

'Yes? What is it?'

'We're going to get your wife into a cubicle where she can lie down—'

'And who are you?' he demanded.

It was not a surprising question, Sarah decided, since she was wearing a faded pair of jeans and a

denim shirt which seemed to have shrunk in the
wash. Either that or her weight gain was more
serious than she had first thought! And, with her
windswept dark hair spilling untidily over her
shoulders, she looked more like a backpacking
student than a nurse!

'I'm a qualified midwife; I work here at
Southbury Hospital,' she told him calmly, hoping
that her voice carried more authority than her
appearance. 'I think that your wife would be happier in the privacy of a cubicle, don't you? I'm
going to stay with her until she's safely upstairs
in the labour ward. Can you please tell me your
wife's name?'

The man's face lost a little of its strained,
desperate quality. 'It's Cathy. Cathy Morris. And
I'm Jack.'

Sarah nodded then crouched down so that she
was able to gently take the woman's hand in hers
and look her in the eye. 'Cathy,' she said softly,
'my name is Sarah Jackson. I'm a midwife and
I'm going to stay with you for a while. We're
going to take you somewhere where you can lie
down.' And there would be a snowball's chance
in hell of finding a spare trolley let alone a porter
to push it, thought Sarah grimly. 'Do you think
you could manage to walk if you lean on me and
your husband?'

'Yes,' groaned the woman. 'I—think so.'

Getting her to cubicle three seemed to take for
ever since Mrs Morris had to keep stopping whenever a contraction rendered her incapable of

walking. Sarah was surreptiously timing the contractions, slightly horrified but not really surprised
to find that they were coming about every two
minutes. Dear goodness! She hoped to heaven that
the obstetrician could move quickly—and even if
he could, she would lay very favourable odds on
him delivering the baby in the accident and emergency department and *not* on Labour Ward!

'Right,' said Sarah, once the three of them were
inside and she had drawn the cubicle curtains.
'Let's get you up on the couch, shall we, Cathy?'

'Oh-h-h!' groaned Cathy, and her arms clutched
helplessly at the swollen bulge of her abdomen.

Sarah and Mr Morris had just got Cathy up onto
the couch and covered her with a sheet when a
harassed-looking staff nurse appeared, her plastic
apron smeared with half-dried blood and her hair
falling down all around her face. She was also
slightly out of breath. 'Thanks for helping out,'
she gasped. 'It's chaos out there! The obstetrician
is on his way—'

But Sarah wasn't listening because the woman
had begun to grunt in the primitive and helpless
way familiar to every midwife the world over. This
woman was about to have her baby no matter what!
'Oh, my goodness, she's pushing!' she announced.
'Someone get me a delivery pack! *Quickly*!'

'Coming right up!' responded the staff nurse in
alarm, scooting out of the cubicle at speed.

Sarah lifted up the sheet and glanced down at
Cathy to see whether the head had made an appear-

ance or 'crowned', as it was known in the profession. She frowned.

Mr Morris saw her expression and said immediately, 'Is everything all right, Staff?'

'So far so good,' answered Sarah smoothly, though tiny beads of sweat were prickling on her brow as she looked down at Cathy again, who was indeed about to deliver a baby very shortly. But instead of being able to see the baby's head Sarah could only see two buttocks, which meant only one thing. . .

'This is a breech!' she exclaimed urgently. 'I need help!' She slammed the flat of her palm on the emergency button.

Immediately a loud alarm began to sound and to Sarah's intense relief the staff nurse ran back in carrying a delivery pack, her eyes flicking anxiously to Sarah's white face as she handed the pack over. 'What's up?'

'Breech birth,' replied Sarah succinctly, not underestimating the problems for a moment. A breech delivery was one where the baby came down the birth canal the wrong way—that is, bottom first instead of head first. There were many attendant risks but the major risk was of death to the baby. The cervix needed to be fully dilated to stop the head getting stuck in the birth canal. Even in controlled conditions a breech delivery was never easy but here, without any of the specialised equipment or qualified experts around. . .

'Where the hell is the obstetrician?' demanded the staff nurse urgently but Sarah shook her head.

'We can't wait for him. This baby won't wait.' She bent her head down to speak to Cathy. 'Your baby is coming now, Cathy, and it's coming bottom first. Do you understand?'

'Y-yes!' gasped Cathy.

Sarah spoke very calmly and slowly. 'Cathy, I want you to listen to me very carefully. You must not push until I've examined you. Do you understand?'

'Yes!' gasped Cathy again and then nearly drew blood as a contraction gripped her and her nails bit hard into Sarah's hand.

Sarah took Cathy's hand in hers and gave it a tight, reassuring squeeze, though inside she was reduced to jelly! But she deliberately pushed away thoughts of all the potential dangers involved and instead concentrated on putting into action all that she had learned, one of the first being to inform the patient without alarming her.

'However much you get the urge—*don't push*!' she reiterated. 'I need to check that your cervix is fully dilated before we let the shoulders slip through.'

'So, what can I do?' demanded the staff nurse. 'I haven't got *any* O and G experience!'

Sarah swallowed, taking a moment for her thoughts to gather some semblance of order. Like most midwives, even the really experienced ones, she had never delivered a breech baby and there was one simple reason for that—the doctors always did them!

'We need to get her to the end of the bed,' instructed Sarah. '*Now*!'

With the help of Jack Morris, Sarah and the staff nurse helped to lift Cathy to the end of the bed, though it wasn't easy.

'OK!' puffed Sarah. 'Let's get her bottom right on the edge of the bed. That's it! Now, I want you two to hold her legs up and back slightly. Bent at the knee like this, right?'

'Right!' her assistants chorused.

'I want you to do everything I tell you,' instructed Sarah, 'so that we can deliver a healthy, bouncing baby! Give me those gloves, would you, Staff?'

'Sure.'

Sarah swiftly pulled on the latex gloves. 'Just going to examine you now, Cathy.' She pushed her hand up, checking that she could not feel the cervix. 'You're fully dilated!' she declared triumphantly. 'You can start pushing now!'

Cathy closed her eyes in concentration and grunted with the effort.

'That's it, darling,' cooed her husband. 'Just like that!'

'You're doing brilliantly, Cathy,' said Sarah encouragingly as she waited anxiously for the neck to appear before she delivered the head, praying inwardly that an uncontrolled delivery of the head would not lead to intracranial haemmorhage and the death of the baby.

She didn't notice a white-coated figure appear

in the cubicle and silently observe her progress with a sharp-eyed scrutiny.

However, the staff nurse who was hanging onto one of Cathy's legs *did* notice Southbury's most eligible bachelor and said, 'Oh, *there* you are, Mr Brennan! Thank goodness for that!'

Pausing for a second, Sarah lifted her head and gave him a questioning look. 'Do you want to take over?'

He was professional enough not to let his answer be guided by the fact that he fancied her like hell. He had seen enough to make him shake his head and say confidently, 'You're doing just fine. I'm here if you need me.'

She nodded. 'Push *now*, would you, Cathy?' Sarah instructed. 'A really big, hard push.' And just at that moment the head appeared and Sarah's arms reached out automatically to catch the baby, overwhelmingly relieved to see that it was a healthy pink colour and seemingly not at all affected by its traumatic journey down the birth canal.

'It's a boy!' she shouted exuberantly as the boy in question let out the first lusty yell of his life. 'A beautiful, bouncing baby boy!'

After the cord had been cut and tied, the baby cleaned and swaddled and awaiting the paediatrician, there were the usual post-birth experiences, which varied from parent to parent. But this was a first baby and first babies were extra-special, thought Sarah, beaming with delight as she looked around the over-crowded cubicle. The tears of joy and relief, the slight awkwardness of the new father handling the tiny scrap. The twinned elation and exhaustion of the mother.

And the midwife, decided Sarah, rubbing the back of a newly washed hand across her forehead and blinking as she realised that it was past midnight.

A stunningly attractive Indian woman in a sister's uniform popped her head around the curtain and beamed at the baby. 'Whoopee!' she said in delight. 'First baby born in A and E since *I've* been Sister. My heartfelt congratulations to you both,' she told the proud parents softly.

'Thanks,' said Jack, looking down at his wife who was tenderly suckling their newborn son.

'And to you, Staff,' said Sister, her eyes twinkling at Sarah. 'You acted commendably. Although Mr Brennan tells me that it really was beyond the call of duty—since you don't actually start work until Monday morning!'

Sarah bit her lip. 'I didn't mean—'

'We're all very proud of you,' said Sister quietly. 'Very proud. Aren't we, Jamie?'

'Absolutely,' murmured Jamie, wishing that he could be alone with her for a moment.

A blond-haired man in a white coat, who was obviously the casualty officer, loomed up behind Sister. 'Calls for some of that champagne you've been stashing in your room since Christmas, don't you think, Sister?' he grinned.

'Run along and get some, then,' Sister instructed sweetly. 'You, of all people, know where the glasses are!'

Across the room Sarah's eyes met the dazzling blue flames of Jamie Brennan's dancing gaze and she did her best to remain cool.

'Well done,' he said, coming over to stand beside her. He must have been a little over six feet and Sarah realised just what a powerful physique he had—all tight and honed musculature and healthy limbs. For some reason it was even more noticeable beneath the crisp starchiness of the white coat he wore than it had been when he had been half-naked in the swimming pool earlier. Or perhaps it was simply that Sarah now knew what a devastating body was hidden by his doctor's coat. . .

His blue eyes crinkled at the corners as he smiled and remaining unmoved was becoming more difficult by the second, Sarah realised.

'That was a perfect breech delivery I witnessed just now,' he told her gravely, and the unmistakable admiration in his eyes told Sarah that he was not being facetious.

She went pink with pride. 'Thank you,' she said quietly.

'My pleasure,' he answered in quite a different voice altogether. There was an undeniable flash of desire in the blue eyes, which was swiftly replaced by a mocking question. And Sarah's bubble of delight burst immediately as vivid recollections of the afternoon appeared in glorious Technicolor in her mind's eye, as though her memory was determined to remind her that he had a life which could never include her. She did not *want* him flirting with her. Did she? He had a wife and a child and she would do well to remember that.

And so would he.

She made to turn away, her face chilly and expressionless. 'Please excuse me,' she said stiffly. 'I'd like to accompany Cathy up to the postnatal ward.'

'Sure,' shrugged Jamie, slightly taken aback. What the hell had he *said*? One minute she was all flushed and breathless and smiling at him in a way which had quite taken his breath away, the pleasure in her slanting green eyes shining out like a beacon.

And the next?

Her face had become an icy, unrecognisable mask. He frowned, about to say something more when the paediatrician arrived to check the baby over. Leander Le Saux was a world expert on cystic fibrosis and a keen squash player; he and Jamie played together when both their tight schedules allowed—which wasn't very often.

'Hi, Jamie,' he smiled. 'Turning our department into a delivery room, are you? *And* a breech birth, I hear?'

'Oh, I didn't deliver him,' replied Jamie, his eyes fixed on the dark-haired girl who was bent over Cathy Morris, laughing as she said something, her dark hair all shiny and mussed. 'One of our new midwives did the honour.'

Something in the way he spoke made Leander give him a long, hard look as he followed the direction of Jamie's eyes, slightly surprised to see a casually clad young woman in denim. Leander was a happily married man and madly in love with his stunning young wife, Nicolette, but even he could clearly see the girl's attraction. And so, quite obviously, could Jamie, he thought with amusement.

Leander gave a small smile as he walked over to introduce himself to the new baby's parents. Wait until he told Nicolette about this, he thought; she had been trying to pair Jamie Brennan off for ages!

CHAPTER FOUR

SARAH unlocked the door to her room, went inside and stood for a moment at the uncurtained window, staring out at the Southbury skyline. In the distance the silver sliver of moon sent down a pale and oddly ghostly radiance, illuminating the main spire of the cathedral so that it rose up in relief like a giant pencil dominating the night sky.

It was way past one o'clock. She had left a tired but exuberant Cathy Morris on the postnatal ward and had then trooped off back down to Accident and Emergency to sit with Mick while he awaited the result of his X-ray. It then transpired that Mick had indeed fractured his wrist in what was known as a Colles' fracture. Setting it in plaster was a relatively simple procedure but it needed to be done under a general anaesthetic, which could never be given to a patient with a full stomach because of the risk of food being vomited and then inhaled into the lungs.

Because Mick fell into the category of having a full stomach—having drunk four pints of beer and then eaten an enormous curry—the orthopaedic surgeons told him that they would be unable to operate until the following morning.

'I've got to be admitted to the orthopaedic ward,' he told Sarah rather plaintively.

Sarah had felt slightly guilty then for the complete lack of sympathy that she had shown towards him. But Mick was tough. And gorgeous. And no doubt would have half the nurses on the ward rushing to do his every whim!

In her room Sarah drew the curtains and shut out the cathedral spire, snapped the light on and stripped her clothes off. She donned a towelling bathrobe and padded off down the corridor to the bathroom.

After a shower and hair-wash she felt clean and fresh but annoyingly wide awake. She put on the pair of jade-green satin pyjamas that Benedict and Verity had given her last Christmas and sat down on the bed. She knew that she *should* feel tired but, quite frankly, sleep was the last thing on her mind.

She glanced around the bare room. She really must unpack first thing tomorrow. At least with all her things and little knick-knacks around her it might look a little bit more like home and less like a prison cell!

Sarah swallowed back a suspiciously salty lump in her throat. She had never lived away from her parents before and waves of homesickness began to wash over her.

She tried to tell herself that everything would look brighter in the morning and that she should be feeling elated after successfully delivering a breech baby in such difficult circumstances.

But it was no good. Her normal sunny nature stubbornly refused to show itself.

Frustrated, Sarah got up and began foraging

around in one of her bags for the bottle of sherry her mother had thrust into her hands just before she had left home.

She wasn't sure what kind of circumstances her mother had *expected* her to live in, she thought with a hint of wry amusement as she hunted around in the kitchen cupboard to find a glass which was not chipped, but they sure were basic!

She had just poured herself two fingers of the finest amontillado her father's cellar could provide when there was a soft tap on the door and Sarah looked at it blankly. Must be another nurse with insomnia, she thought. And I could badly do with some company.

Putting her untouched glass down on the coffee-table, she strode over to the door and pulled it open to discover Jamie Brennan standing there. Her heart began slamming frantically against her chest and a delicious excitement began to steal over her skin. And it didn't seem to matter how much she told herself that he was off limits—that bubbly feeling of excitement simply would not go away.

His first words, however, completely floored her. 'Do you always answer the door so readily at this time of night?' he demanded.

There was a brief moment when she considered slamming the aforementioned door in his handsome face but Sarah was far too well brought up to do anything as melodramatic as that. As it was, his outrageous question was just what she needed to bring her right back to her senses.

'And why the hell shouldn't I?' she retorted.

'Because it could be *anyone*—that's why!' His eyes sparked blue fire as his gaze raked reluctantly over the healthy curves of her body. Lord, but she was a vision in those green pyjamas that matched her eyes so perfectly! 'There are all kinds of strange people who take to hanging around nurses' homes!'

'So I see,' she countered, tongue in cheek.

'Don't do it again!'

He gave the order as though he had every right to do so, Sarah thought, her natural indignation rising like smoke from a bonfire. 'If I'd known it was you,' she said deliberately, 'then I wouldn't have answered!'

He stared at her consideringly. 'So, aren't you going to invite me in?'

'What for?'

It was a question which Jamie could not answer truthfully because he honestly did not know why he was here. He had not stopped to question his motives for knocking on her door and part of him was not sure that he even wanted to.

He saw the emerald light of challenge in her slanting eyes and some answering response stirred deep within him—a response that he did not dare to analyse, although instinct told him that it was a response he had thought dead for ever.

'I've just done a particularly tricky forceps delivery on Labour Ward and I was on my way home. I saw your light on and I thought that maybe your adrenalin was high—you know—after your *magnificent* delivery,' he smiled, flirting for the first time in years and finding it exceptionally easy.

Sarah liked him very much but she was no push-over. She raised dark, quizzical brows. 'And you, of course, just *happened* to be passing my room in the nurses' home?'

He met her bold stare with one of his own. 'No,' he admitted softly. 'I didn't.'

'So how did you know where I lived?' she quizzed curiously.

Jamie's mouth quirked slightly at the corners but he didn't look in the least bit abashed. 'I asked at Reception,' he murmured. 'Your name was on your—er—friend's casualty card,' he added, his eyes becoming very blue and narrowing for a moment as he jealously remembered the curly-haired man she had been with earlier in A and E. And he had been rather horrified at his pleased reaction on discovering that that same man was at present a patient on the orthopaedic ward!

'Oh, I see.' Sarah bit back a comment of bewilderment. So he had made an effort to seek her out, had he?

The air was fraught with tension and Sarah was at a loss what to do or say next. She stared at him rather helplessly, wishing that she knew a bit more about men. For a twenty-five-year-old she was painfully lacking in experience and what she knew about the opposite sex could have been written on the back of a postage stamp!

'You haven't answered my question, Sarah,' he murmured.

'I've forgotten what your question was,'

answered Sarah huskily. And it was true. With those dazzling blue eyes fixed on her face like that she was in danger of forgetting her own name!

'I asked whether you were going to invite me in?'

Not until she had got one thing straight, she thought, and she didn't care whether or not it was the 'right' thing to ask—she needed to know. 'Are you married?' she asked bluntly.

Jamie was surprised. And flattered. He had had women quiz him about his marital status before. But never with such refreshing honesty or lack of guile. And such candour deserved a similar response. 'No,' he smiled widely. 'I'm not married.'

'So the little girl I saw you with earlier—?'

'Is my daughter. The young woman who was with us is Marianne, her nanny,' he elaborated.

So he was divorced. She let the sigh of relief out as slowly as she could so that he wouldn't hear it. And strangely, it didn't occur for her to doubt him for a moment. Because she knew, with an inner certainty, that Jamie Brennan would never lie to her. Quite how she knew that, she wasn't sure—but she did!

She held the door open wider. 'You'd better come in.'

Jamie walked in and the first thing he saw was Mick's motorbike helmet on the floor and his face tightened, his mouth curving with a disdain that he could not disguise. It seemed that it was now *his* turn for candour, only he found the words spilling out of his mouth in an aggressive way which was frighteningly unfamiliar to him. 'Where's your boyfriend?' he fired out roughly.

Sarah blinked with bewilderment until she saw in which direction his eyes were looking. 'Oh, that,' she said, rather flippantly. 'It's Mick's. He won't be needing it tonight. They've admitted him to the orthopod ward; he's got a Colles' fracture.'

Jamie felt a murderous rage envelop him. 'And if he hadn't inconveniently fractured his wrist?' he demanded. 'Would he now be enjoying the comforts of your bed?'

Sarah was astounded. And furious. Not as furious as she would have been if any other man had made such an outrageous suggestion but furious enough. 'G-get out of here,' she told him, her voice shaking with anger. 'I don't have to listen to that kind of tacky insult.'

By now Jamie had calmed down and he was as horrified as Sarah clearly was. 'I'm sorry,' he said simply. 'I had no right to say that. No right at all. Please forgive me.'

With a melting blue stare like that he could have brought a statue to life, thought Sarah, wondering what the correct code was for entertaining men at this time of night! 'He's not my boyfriend,' she told him. 'He's just a friend from my last hospital.'

'Good!' Jamie beamed.

Sarah was unprepared for the look of immense pleasure that greeted her remark about Mick and, unsure of what to do next, she gestured rather nervously towards her glass of sherry. 'I was just having a drink. Would you like one?'

'Please.'

She found another glass, tipped a generous slug of the golden brown liquid into it and handed it over.

'Thanks,' he said appreciatively as he took the glass and sipped it from it. 'Mmm. That's good.'

'Won't you sit down?' Sarah suggested formally, realising that she sounded frighteningly like her mother as she did so!

Jamie looked around the room. There was some sort of bed-settee or a hard chair on offer. He chose the chair and sipped at his drink again. Now that he was actually here, he wasn't quite sure *what* to do. He felt like the prince who had wakened the sleeping beauty after a hundred years of sleep. The trouble was—what did the prince do next? The fairy tale never really explained beyond that. Perhaps it was best not to. It would, after all, be a bit of a let-down to the reader if the prince's next words to his princess were, 'Did you sleep well?'

Sarah stared at him, noticing for the first time the tiny lines which fanned his blue eyes and the lean angles of jaw and his high cheek-bones— seeing a face that looked as though it had seen more than its fair share of tension. She wondered what had happened to Jamie Brennan in the past. Where was his wife now?

He looked up into those interested and compassionate green eyes and suddenly found that he wanted to tell her. Everything.

'My wife is dead,' he said baldly as if he could

read her thoughts, nodding his dark head at Sarah's shocked inrush of breath at his words. He was used to the horror and the disbelief. Young mothers did not die. But they did. Oh, they did. He began to recite the facts in the matter-of-fact manner he had practised in his head for months after Kathy's death. Words he had hardly been able to bear to use, except to the very few. And yet he found it surprisingly easy to tell them to Sarah.

'Yes. She developed a brain tumour—a meningioma—which can be cured but. . . Kathy was one of the unlucky ones,' he added painstakingly. 'The prognosis was poor from the beginning.'

As though the medical detail was somehow important, thought Sarah, keeping her eyes from brimming over with sympathy only with a huge effort.

'It happened when Harriet was only two,' he continued painfully, his handsome face becoming ravaged with the memory. 'Kathy died two years later. But we managed to keep her at home all that time—that was somehow terribly important to all of us. That she die surrounded by her family, in her own bed, not in some anonymous hospital ward amongst strangers. You know?'

'Yes, I know,' she answered quietly. Well, fortunately, she didn't actually know. But she could imagine.

He took a deep swallow of the sherry, his eyes unseeing as they stared into the middle distance. 'We were obviously expecting it to happen but it still came as a terrible shock—death always does. And, of course, it was particularly hard for Harriet.'

'And for you?' Sarah prompted softly. 'So hard for you, too, surely? Having to be brave for Harriet's sake. Holding onto your sanity enough to try to keep the family going. And your job, of course. Holding that down with any degree of competence. It must have been very hard indeed.'

He looked at her with tremendous gratitude, shaken to the core by the depth of her understanding. It was now almost five years since Kathy's death and he had gone out briefly with other women; of course he had. But, apart from Verity, the experience had been a sobering one. It seemed that women could be desperately jealous of the love he had shared with his wife. And it seemed that even acknowledging that love could represent a kind of betrayal. Ludicrous. Jealousy from women on the make—whom he had scarcely known for five minutes. It had sickened him.

Her eyes were still soft with sympathy but not the kind of cloying sympathy which could grate so easily on nerves already stretched to breaking point. Some of the tension drifted out of him and the broad line of his shoulders unconsciously relaxed. 'Hard for me, too,' he admitted, and put his empty glass down on the well-worn carpet. 'God, but you're understanding,' he told her frankly, staring at her intently as though it was the very first time that he had seen her. 'So very understanding.'

She shook her head. 'Not usually,' she said, then took a sip of her sherry, embarrassed by his undisguised admiration and afraid that her words might make her sound too pushy. Or too noble. She lifted her chin up. 'Anyway,' she told him honestly, 'I'm not so terribly understanding underneath; not really. I'm afraid I jumped to the conclusion that you were divorced.' She stared at him defiantly as if expecting censure but none came.

'Of course you did,' he said gently. 'Why on earth should you think otherwise?'

She saw vulnerability written in the soft, sensual lines of his mouth and Sarah's heart went out to him. Without stopping to think of how he would interpret her action, she patted the space beside her on the bed-settee. 'Why don't you come and sit here?' she invited, recovering enough to justify it with an added, 'That chair looks jolly uncomfortable.'

He smiled, now feeling relaxed enough in her company to do just that, but when he was seated beside her he wondered whether he had done the right thing because he became acutely aware of just how tantalisingly the slippery satin fell over and clung to the lush curves of her breasts. And of the fresh, newly washed scent that came delicately off her skin. He felt strangely nervous and if he hadn't been on call he might have asked for another sherry. But since when did he ever have to start seeking courage in alcohol?

Since about fifteen minutes ago—that's when!

The gorgeous Jamie looked as nervous as *she* did, Sarah thought, and decided that it was time to practise her conversational skills! 'So, what brought you to Southbury?' she asked, leaning back to relax once her own empty glass had joined his on the carpet. 'Or are you from this part of the world originally?'

'No, I'm not. I came here about a year ago,' he told her, realising that now was not the right time to talk about Verity and the influence she had had in changing the direction of his life. Sarah had already been more than understanding about Kathy but it might be stretching her goodwill a little too much if he then confided about another woman he had been close to!

So, instead, he concentrated on all the fundamental reasons why he had chosen to leave a busy London teaching hospital to come to the south coast of England.

'I was working in London when Kathy was first diagnosed,' he told her, 'and so we stayed put. We needed to; we needed the support system of all the friends we had there.' He automatically thought of Verity and of what a godsend she had been, taking Harriet off their hands whenever they needed her to. And how close Harriet had grown to Sammi, Verity's daughter. For a while they had been more like sisters than friends.

'After Kathy died I just carried on without thinking, really. Then Harriet was due to start school but the local schools were very big and she was still feeling very raw and after a while I started feeling that she was in danger of sinking without a trace.'

He stared down at his hands. 'Also, after the initial shock of Kathy's death, I was forced to re-evaluate my circumstances. I had to think to myself, did I really want to spend the rest of my life living in a large, anonymous city? Was that what I wanted for Harriet?' He shrugged, then clasped his long surgeon's fingers together. 'The answer was an emphatic ''no'',' he smiled, noticing that parts of her hair were still damp from the shower and that the dark, glossy locks were drying with just the hint of a kink in them.

'Then, quite by chance, I got the job offer from Southbury. The chance to run my very own department which, incidentally, was much better funded than in my last post. It seemed almost as though fate was intervening. And when we came to look at the place and Harriet saw that she could have a decent-sized garden *and* live by the sea then, well. . .' and he grinned and shrugged '. . .there was really no contest.'

'Sounds perfect,' murmured Sarah.

'Mmm,' he agreed, and watched her from beneath the shield of the thick, black lashes that framed his dazzling blue eyes. Was there something dutiful in her reply? he wondered. With a flash of insight Jamie realised that he was in great danger here. Of becoming the noble and untouchable widower in Sarah's eyes. And he did not want her to think of him as untouchable, he realised. That was the last thing on his mind.

So he could now do one of two things. He could politely take his leave of her. Thank her for the sherry and head for the door, maybe pausing there to ask whether she would have dinner with him some time.

Or he could kiss her.

He leaned lazily towards her, giving her all the time in the world to stop his lips from seeking hers but there was no need. Sarah had turned towards him eagerly, her mouth already parted and her hands reaching to hold onto his shoulders, as if for support.

He had not kissed a woman for a long time. Indeed, he wasn't sure whether he had ever kissed a woman in quite the same way as he now kissed Sarah. Not even Kathy. He was thirty-three years old and the years of abstinence had sharpened his sexual appetite so that he now felt as if he was enmeshed in the sweetest trap imaginable.

'Oh, Sarah,' he murmured against her mouth, which tasted of toothpaste and sherry, the scent of her newly-washed hair invading his nostrils. 'Beautiful, beautiful Sarah.' And he kissed her again.

Sarah had *never* been kissed like this before and she almost fainted with pleasure in his arms. It was as though she had entered an entirely new dimension, she thought as she struggled to make sense of it all through the hazy waters of desire. One where nothing existed except feeling and sensation and a growing awareness that kissing was simply not enough. Not enough at all. That it had to lead onto something else—something infinitely better. And that Jamie seemed very sure about which path to take.

So that when he slowly unbuttoned her pyjama jacket and began to stroke one breast with tantalising fingers, which promised even as they excited, she was incapable of doing anything other than shuddering with pleasure and praying that he wouldn't stop.

'Do you like that?' he whispered.

'Oh, yes, yes,' she breathed ecstatically, the words torn from her mouth. 'Please don't stop!'

He gave a husky kind of laugh. 'Oh, no, sweet Sarah. Believe me when I tell you that I have no intention of stopping.'

Jamie awoke in confusion, his senses immediately telling him that he was surrounded by the unfamiliar. He felt the softness of something nestling sweetly against his palm and realised that his hand still cupped Sarah's breast.

He looked down at her sleeping beauty and stifled a groan of guilt and dismay.

What the hell had he *done*?

He released her with difficulty; the bed was cramped, designed by monastic architects to accommodate just one person. Only their bare thighs were interlocked now. He tentatively shifted his leg and stared sightlessly up at the ceiling.

How *could* he have done it? he asked himself with growing horror. Made love to her so swiftly—and not even used any protection?

But that had not been the worst of it—she had
been a *virgin*, for heaven's sake! Although he
would never have guessed it, not from her passionate response to him on the bed-settee. And he had
never made love to a virgin before. Even Kathy had
had some sexual experience before they had met.

Sickened by the stale taste of self-disgust, he
lifted his wrist up to see the time, closing his eyes
in despair to see that it was almost six o'clock.

He had to get back before Harriet woke up. He
had to!

As he crept around finding his scattered clothes
in the pale light of dawn which filtered through
the curtains he didn't stop to reason with himself
that he had come in later than this many times.
Times when he had been stuck with an awkward
delivery on the labour ward or doing an emergency
Caesarean or operating on a woman with a suspected ectopic pregnancy.

Guilt clung to his skin like coal dust as he wondered how he would ever be able to face his
daughter without feeling that in some way he had
betrayed the memory of her mother.

CHAPTER FIVE

Monday morning.

Sarah did up the last button of her uniform, looked in the mirror and grimaced. Not so much at her appearance—though her hair had stubbornly refused to lie flat and her dark blue dress clung to every lush curve in what she considered a very unflattering way. Or even at the earliness of the hour—after all, as a nurse she was quite used to getting up at the crack of dawn. It was just that she was used to doing it on more than a totally sleepless night!

No, the reason for her grimace was her anticipated meeting with Jamie, the man into whose arms she had so eagerly fallen the night before last.

And who had crept out without a word or a note. Nothing.

She had woken up in crumpled sheets to survey the empty space beside her with disbelief, her body still tingling from the deep, achingly new sensations he had aroused.

Like an abandoned puppy she had clung onto every last hope, telling herself that maybe he had been bleeped away on an emergency and that she had been sleeping too deeply for him to be able to rouse her.

She had even, pathetically, hung around her flat

all the following day just in case he had wanted to get in touch with her.

He hadn't, of course. Only it had taken some time for the unpalatable truth to hit her with all the force of a sledgehammer. For hadn't her mother told her time and time again that men never respected a woman who was 'easy'? And, dear heavens, you couldn't get much 'easier' than she had been! She had only known him for less than a day and he hadn't even had to go to the trouble of taking her out to supper. She had given him a glass of her father's best sherry in something resembling a toothmug, had listened to his life story and then had tumbled into bed with him.

Sarah pinned her hospital badge onto the front of her dark blue dress as she thought about how she was going to face him on the ward today.

She glanced down at her fob watch, sick to the stomach at the thought of having to maintain a professional relationship with him after what had happened between them.

She felt moody and out of sorts and more in need of a restorative cup of strong, black coffee before starting work than she had ever been before. The irony was that she was going to have to do without. She didn't actually *have* any coffee because she had moped around in the flat all day instead of doing the sensible thing and going out to buy a few provisions for herself. And even if she had known where the canteen was she didn't feel up to confronting a sea of unfamiliar faces.

But then she caught a horrified glimpse of her

pale, woebegone face in the mirror and drew herself up short.

Honestly, Sarah Jackson, she chided herself with a touch of her usual spirit, you have *not* started as you mean to go on! So what was she going to do next? Make herself a doormat? Act like a victim?

No way!

She had already made one big mistake and she did not intend making another! She was *not* going to stare longingly at Jamie Brennan, reminding herself what a great lover he was. She was going to be the epitome of brisk, cool efficiency. After all, he was obviously regretting what had happened as much as she was, otherwise why would he have just disappeared like that? So, if she had any sense in her head she would do well to forget the whole thing.

On the way to work Sarah called into the orthopaedic ward to find Mick. Just as she had expected, he was propped up on a bank of pillows with his arm in plaster and an extremely pretty nurse actually popping a grape into his mouth! Sarah could have groaned. Talk about subservient! She sat down on the bed and took a grape herself.

'How's it going?' she queried, her mouth full.

He held up his plastered wrist. 'OK. They operated yesterday. I felt pretty grim after the anaesthetic—'

'Must have been all that beer and curry,' said Sarah unsympathetically.

'They're letting me out today. My bike is fixed

but I can't drive it home, obviously. So one of the nurses is running me back home after she's finished today.' His devastating golden brown eyes glimmered. 'I'll come back and collect the bike when my wrist is fixed.' He stared at Sarah closely. 'So, what's up with you?'

Sarah blanched. Mick might appear wild but he was an acutely sensitive man when he chose to be—it was one of the reasons why he was such a brilliant doctor. 'What do you mean?'

'Oh, come *on*, Sarah,' he chided. 'Pinched face. Shadowed eyes. Trembling lips. All adds up to heartbreak, I'm afraid, babe! Who is it—the guy in A and E?'

'None of your business!' she mumbled.

'True,' he mused. 'But if you want a bit of advice from an old hand *don't* let him see he's getting to you. Understand?'

Sarah grinned. He was absolutely right! 'Message understood,' she agreed.

Filled with resolution, Sarah arrived in the maternity unit early and went straight along to Sister's office where she found Sister Singleton sitting at her desk, busily writing up what looked like the midwives' off-duty.

She glanced up when Sarah entered and fixed her with a curious look and for a moment Sarah wondered, rather hysterically, whether the fact that she had lost her virginity was actually visible on her face. What on earth would this respectable-looking middle-aged woman say if she knew that her new staff midwife had leapt into bed with the consultant when she was barely acquainted with him?

'Hello, Sister,' said Sarah as cheerfully as she could. 'I'm Sarah Jackson, your new staff midwife.'

'That's right,' said Sister Singleton, with a nod. 'Met you on Saturday, didn't I? Holding onto Jamie Brennan's hand like a drowning woman!'

Sarah flushed an unbecoming brick-red and wished that the floor would swallow her up. 'It wasn't—I mean, we weren't—'

'Oh, good heavens!' interrupted Sister immediately, appalled by the stricken look that had suddenly appeared on the girl's face at her thoughtless comment. 'I was only teasing you, my dear. Please don't take any notice of me.'

'I—I'm sorry,' said Sarah, in a wobbly voice. 'I d-don't know w-what's got into me.'

Sister Singleton might have been a spinster but she was not stupid. I bet I do, she thought grimly and if Jamie Brennan had arrived at that moment to do his ward round she would have found it exceedingly difficult to be civil to him.

Oh, she was delighted that Jamie was obviously shaking off his grief enough to get involved with other women but heartily displeased that he should have selected her newest member of staff to do it with. Especially if the young woman in question was going to haunt her department with dark-shadowed eyes and a soft mouth that should have been laughing and not trembling with sadness.

However, Sister Singleton decided that this was

one of those occasions when turning a blind eye
was the best solution. 'Probably because it's hot
and high summer, my dear,' she told Sarah airily.
'Also, you're starting a new job, don't forget,
which is always a little stressful. And I believe
you've only just qualified?'

With an effort Sarah pulled herself together.
'That's right. Just two and a half weeks ago. This
is my first proper job.'

'And we'll make sure that your time here is
an exceedingly happy one!' said Sister Singleton
determinedly.

'Thank you, Sister,' said Sarah, hoping that the
doubt that assailed her did not show on her face.

'Now, what I normally do with my new midwives is get them to accompany me for the first
week or two—that's if I've got enough staff on,
mind you!' said Sister jokingly. 'And the amazing
thing is that this week I *do* have enough staff! I'll
be buzzing between antenatal and postnatal wards,
as well as the labour ward, so just stick close to
my side! That way you'll get to see how I like the
entire department to be run and you'll meet all the
staff. Once you've found your feet I will allocate
you to one of the three wards and you will do a
four-month internal rotation on each. How does
that sound to you?'

'It sounds wonderful, Sister,' said Sarah fervently.

Sister's fine grey eyes crinkled up at the corners
as she smiled at the eager expression on Sarah's
face. 'You weren't expecting anything so revolu-

tionary in a provincial hospital?' she guessed drily. 'Such things only happen in London, right?'

Sarah grinned. 'Actually, where I trained that would be considered *far* too revolutionary. You never know—the nurses might get to expect such reasonable treatment!'

Sister laughed. 'And where exactly did you train?'

'St Thomas's.'

'Ah!'

'You know it, Sister?'

'Who doesn't? I worked there once a long time ago.' Her grey eyes took on a wistful, faraway expression. 'Good hospital but a little on the formal side, if I might say so!' She glanced down at the fob watch that lay over her comfortable-looking bosom. 'You're terribly early, my dear!'

'That's new-girl-itis,' responded Sarah with a smile. 'I won't always be like this.'

'Thank heavens for that!' said Sister, smiling broadly. 'Or you would give me something to have to live up to! The rest of the day staff won't breeze in until dead on half past seven so why don't you pop along to the kitchen and make us both a cup of coffee? I like mine white—with three sugars, please. Oh, and my cup is the orange one with ''I'm a mug from Southbury'' written on the side!'

'Yes, Sister. Thank you, Sister,' said Sarah as she sped off towards the kitchen, thinking that her immediate superior looked as though she was going to turn out to be a very decent sort altogether!

She was carefully bringing the two cups towards

the office when, as she approached, she heard the sound of a deep, male voice and both her hands trembled so much that she had to stop, struggling to control her breathing and attempting to steady her hands.

For that was Jamie's voice; there was no doubt about that. She would have recognised it anywhere and at any time, even though it had not actually spoken to her at great length. But, then, how would you ever forget the sound of a voice that had whispered such intimate things in her ears while he was making love to her; that made her blush even now, just thinking about them?

Point one, she told herself. You simply *don't* think about them. Such thoughts are definitely taboo. And point two. He isn't interested. Men who are interested don't bed a woman and then abandon them by creeping out in the middle of the night. Maybe he does that kind of thing a lot, in which case your only defence is to show him that you don't care even if you're breaking up in pieces inside. You've learnt a bitter lesson, Sarah Jackson, she realised as she compressed her mouth into a straight line and walked steadily towards the office. Make sure he never finds out.

Jamie looked up as Sarah carried the cups into the office and Sarah thought that his face looked guarded.

'Hi!' she said cheerily. 'I'm afraid I didn't know you were here or I'd have made you a coffee.'

Jamie felt like death. He had crept home on Sunday morning to find Harriet already up and oddly suspicious, her suspicions only confirmed when she had rather triumphantly pulled a very long, dark hair from his shirt-sleeve and had then spent an age ostentatiously sniffing the air, having obviously detected Sarah's perfume.

'Have you used a new aftershave, Daddy?' she had asked.

He had supposed it had been his own fault; he might as well have painted the word 'guilt' on his forehead in big, black letters. 'Er—no,' he had muttered, reaching for the coffee percolator.

Harriet had been noisily crunching her cornpops but now had put her spoon down with a look of dogged determination that Jamie had recognised with a sinking heart. 'So, what kept you?' she'd demanded.

'Kept me?' he'd hedged.

Harriet had thrown him a please-don't-play-the-innocent-with-*me* glance. 'Yes, Daddy,' she had answered tartly. 'What kept you? Out all night?'

Jamie had blinked. He'd supposed that other fathers in his situation might have told their nine-year-old daughters to mind their own business. But he had never wanted, nor had had, that kind of repressive relationship with Harriet. They had always been able to talk freely to one another. However, he'd racked his brains for something to tell her which wouldn't have been strictly a lie.

Inspiration had hit him. 'A breech birth!' he'd beamed.

Harriet's amber-brown eyes had narrowed in a frown. 'But Marianne left a note last night saying that there was a breech delivery in A and E. Was there more than one, then?'

'Er—no.'

'It must have been a very *difficult* breech birth, then, Daddy?' had queried Harriet, who had had the rudiments of obstetrics and gynaecology patiently explained to her by her doting father since she'd been knee-high to a grasshopper. 'If it kept you out until this time?'

Jamie had been torn with admiration for his daughter's powers of logic and absolute fury that she should have been subjecting him to the third degree at her relatively tender years! 'I don't want to discuss it!' he had snarled as he'd poured himself a cup of coffee, pleased to see that at least Harriet had had the intelligence and the good sense to know when to let up.

But he had had a tough day with her. Harriet had taken it in turns to sulk and be belligerent and if Jamie hadn't been feeling so guilty about having made love to the first woman since his wife had died then he probably would not have tolerated it. As it was, he'd taken her on a long-promised trip to the zoo and by the time they had got back and he had organised her tea and her bath and settled her into bed and read her a story it had been almost ten o'clock. And far too late to ring Sarah.

Even if he could have thought of what to say to her.

He hadn't imagined what her attitude towards him might be when he did see her again but it certainly wasn't the almost casual air of insouciance she displayed as she breezed into Sister's office, carrying two mugs of coffee.

A dark spear of jealousy shot through him. Maybe she was so used to brief sexual encounters that it was par for the course for her. Until, like the biggest fool in the world, he reminded himself that *he* had been the one to rob her of her innocence.

And back came the guilt.

He stood looking directly at Sarah but all her attention was fixed determinedly on Sister Singleton.

Sister gave Sarah's bright smile an experienced scrutiny. 'Like to come down to the postnatal ward first? See your breech baby?'

'Love to!' beamed Sarah, the brilliant memory of the birth momentarily eclipsing what had happened afterwards in her bedroom. 'How's he doing?'

'Come and see for yourself.'

And Sarah turned her back and walked out of the office without another word or look at Jamie, feeling pleased that she had been able to ignore him quite so effectively. *That* would show him! Mr One-Night-Stand!

Cathy Morris was feeding her son when Sarah and Sister Singleton arrived by the bedside.

'What, *again*?' joked Sister. 'That boy never stops feeding!'

'He seems to have a huge appetite!' laughed Cathy. 'Just like his father!' She stroked the blond-ish down on his head with one long fingertip and looked up to smile into Sarah's eyes. 'Thank you so much for everything you did for me and Jonathon last night.'

'I was only doing my job,' replied Sarah modestly.

Cathy shook her head. 'No, you weren't! I understand that you were off duty?'

'Oh, well,' said Sarah, shrugging with an embarrassed little smile. 'You know what they say about nurses—you're *never* off duty!' She frowned. 'What *I* can't understand, though, is why your husband brought you to A and E in the first place instead of the labour ward. They must have told him what to do in your antenatal classes at the clinic?'

Cathy wrinkled her nose in bemusement as she carefully unhooked Jonathon from one breast with her forefinger and then latched him onto the other nipple, where he began sucking just as lustily.

'Oh, you know what men are!' she giggled. 'He panicked, basically, although to be fair to him I had not expected such a rapid labour—not with a first baby! I thought that I was going to go through the ceiling with the strength of those contractions! And I was in such a state myself that I think if he'd told me that we were going to take a space-shuttle to deliver the baby on Jupiter I would have agreed!'

'You make giving birth sound so appealing,' commented Sarah drily.

'You just wait!' twinkled Cathy.

Sarah was about to make some reply like

'Never!' when the memory of last night hit her like an unexpected shower. She could be pregnant *right now*, she realised with stark horror. She might have been a virgin but she had had a thorough sex education like the next person—and Jamie had not used anything to. . . She swallowed down the lump of distaste in her throat. What on earth would she do if she was?

'Everything all right, Staff?' asked Cathy in a concerned voice. 'You've gone awfully pale.'

Sarah forced a smile. 'First day in a new job!' she joked, realising that she would have to put the fear of pregnancy out of her mind or she would end up not being able to work properly. 'Always slightly stressful!'

'Have a chocolate, then,' coaxed Cathy. 'Give you some energy. And you, Sister—you'll have one, won't you?'

'Better not,' said Sister, patting her rounded stomach with a rueful look. 'Oh, well, then, perhaps just the one!'

'And what about you, Sarah?' asked Cathy with a smile as she held the box out.

They were her favourite Belgian chocolates and Sarah felt so let down and distressed over Jamie that she was extremely tempted. But her fingers wavered over the mocha *crème* truffle for no more than a second as she remembered the fit of her lime-green bikini. She might have lost her virginity to a man who had simply used her but that did not mean that she had to end up looking massively obese! 'No, thank you!' she said firmly.

She and Sister continued going around the post-natal ward, which was where the mothers and babies were housed, and as Sarah smiled at the bunch of happy new mothers nursing their brand-new babies she was reminded just why she had opted to go into midwifery in the first place.

And not just because her big brother Ben, whom she idolised, was an obstetrician although, she had to admit, that did have a *bit* to do with it!

No, Sarah liked the professional autonomy of the speciality; *she* was the practitioner, qualified to make and carry out her own decisions on the patient's care and treatment, and not just the doctor's handmaiden! She also liked working with women and, more importantly, with fit, healthy women!

The postnatal ward was now a hive of activity with mums washing and feeding and changing their babies. And some—usually second-time-around mums—even being organised enough to apply their own make-up and wash their hair!

One particularly glamorous woman with dark red hair was even lying on the floor of her private room doing sit-ups!

'She's only three days post-partum,' explained Sister, 'but she's an actress—appearing in some Shakespeare thing at Southbury Theatre in a few weeks' time. Come and meet her!'

Sister introduced Sarah to all the patients and, naturally, to their new offspring and Sarah's head was spinning from so many names when they came

out of the last cubicle and stood next to the nurses'
station.

'And over there is the ward kitchen,' Sister
pointed. 'There's the sluice, the clinic room and
the doctors' office. Two of the side rooms are
on the far side of the nurses' station—and right
beside it is the room we tend to reserve for
distressed mums.'

Sarah nodded understandingly. The postnatal
ward housed all the women who had had their
babies and mostly it was an extremely happy ward.
But sometimes a woman had to endure the sorrow
of giving birth to a stillborn baby or having a baby
die just days after the birth or having to face the
future of a life spent coping with a severely handi-
capped child. And for these women privacy from
the pitying eyes of others was essential.

'The hospital is running a course in bereavement
counselling later in the autumn,' said Sister. 'You
might be interested in attending. There are a few
places left.'

'I'd like that very much indeed,' answered Sarah
quietly.

Sister nodded her curly grey head approvingly.
'I'll add your name to my list, then.'

Sarah was thoughtful as she followed Sister
along the polished corridor towards the antenatal
ward, where women who were experiencing
complications of pregnancy were admitted for
observation and treatment.

The unit seemed extremely well run and Sister
was obviously quite a go-ahead sort of person with

very up-to-the-minute ideas. And if Sarah refused to let her personal life get any messier than it already had there was no reason why she should not have a fantastic time at Southbury.

'Come and see Mrs Redwood in bed two. She has suffered three miscarriages,' said Sister. 'So we're planning to put in a Shirodkar suture.' Her voice changed very slightly as she said, 'Oh, there's Jamie with her now. Let's go and sit in with them and you can watch him in action. He's so good with the patients; all the women absolutely adore him.'

Behind her fixed smile Sarah gritted her teeth but said nothing as they drew closer to the bed.

Jamie was sitting on the edge of the bed and he glanced up as the two of them approached, giving Sister an outrageously cajoling smile. 'She'll nag me to get off the bed,' he murmured to Mrs Redwood and the patient, who had been looking very pale and tense, relaxed a little.

'I won't,' twinkled Sister, 'but only because it's *him*!'

'You've only recently moved to Southbury, so I understand, Mrs Redwood?' asked Jamie softly.

Mrs Redwood nodded her head. She had big, dark eyes and smooth, dark hair which was tied in a ponytail at her nape. She would have looked serene and madonna-like had it not been for the worry lines that were creasing her white forehead. 'That's right, Mr Brennan. My husband has just been given a transfer from his London office.'

'I've read your notes, of course,' he told her.

'And this is your fourth pregnancy?'

Mrs Redwood winced. 'That's right, Doctor. After the last one they told me that I had an incompetent cervix.' She hesitated. 'No one really explained it to me so that I could understand, though.'

Jamie frowned slightly. He knew the consultant who Mrs Redwood had been under in London— an arrogant man with a self-inflated ego who seemed to take great pleasure from rattling medical jargon off to patients in such a way that they couldn't understand a single word of it!

'Then I'll do my best to make it clear to you,' he told her thoughtfully. 'As you have just said, we are fairly certain that you have what is known as an incompetent cervix. The cervix is, as I am sure you know, the tight band of muscle at the bottom of the womb that dilates when your baby is due to be born.

'But sometimes this happens early on in the pregnancy—as in your case. As your womb enlarges and the baby gets bigger so your cervix is unable to maintain its tone and becomes dilated. And what happened to you was that during the sixteenth to the twentieth week your membranes ruptured prematurely. This was followed by labour pains and the uterus emptying itself completely.'

'So what's to stop that happening this time?' asked Mrs Redwood worriedly.

Jamie smiled. 'Ah! I'm glad you asked me that because there is a very simple and effective form of treatment known as Shirodkar's operation or

Shirodkar's suture. What I intend to do is to take you up to Theatre and to put a purse-string suture around the internal os of your cervix—basically I'm going to sew it up so that the baby can't come through! Not until we want him to, anyway!'

'And then what happens, Doctor?'

'Then you go home. You rest. You eat well. You keep active—lots of fresh air and gentle exercise. You sleep whenever you want to. In other words. . .' and here his blue eyes crinkled as he smiled and Sarah felt her heart automatically quickening in response '. . .you enjoy your pregnancy. Then, when you've reached full term, or thereabouts, we bring you back in, remove the stitch and a normal labour should follow.'

Mrs Redwood opened her dark eyes very wide. 'And it's that simple?'

Jamie nodded as he stood up. 'It's that simple,' he replied with a smile. 'I'll see you in Theatre this afternoon but you won't see me—you'll be sound asleep!'

'Oh, *thank* you, Doctor!' said Mrs Redwood fervently.

The three of them trooped out and went back to the nursing station. Sarah wanted to ask Jamie a question but felt inhibited by what had happened between them on Saturday night. Which was understandable.

But her working life here was going to be limited and intolerable if she was afraid to ask the consultant a question.

Turning expressionless green eyes on him, she

asked, 'You're doing the operation yourself, are you, Mr Brennan?'

Jamie just managed to stop himself from wincing at the chilly tone in her voice. He could see Sister fixing him with that gimlet eye of hers and he did not want her guessing what had happened between him and Sarah—certainly not before he had a chance to resolve it with her. Which didn't look likely, not the way things were going. She had been giving him the cold shoulder all morning. Either frostily ignoring him or, as now, asking him a question but with such a cold, distant look on a face he remembered as beautifully mobile when observed in the act of love.

He felt like taking her in his arms and hauling her up against him and kissing away that icy little expression of distaste but none of those things were possible in the middle of the ward with Sister standing restrainingly between the two of them. So, instead, Jamie composed his face into what he hoped was a benign expression and set about answering Sarah's question as emotionlessly as he could.

'Yes, I'm putting the Shirodkar suture in,' he agreed. 'Does that surprise you?'

He was terribly approachable for a consultant, Sarah thought. That much was evident from the easy way that he responded to her question and tossed back a casual query of his own. But was his approachability anything to do with the fact that he had shared her bed? Sarah cringed inwardly.

'I wondered why—as the consultant, I mean—

you're doing the operation?' She saw the question in his blue eyes and, even though she felt like fleeing as far from his presence as possible, professional pride forced her to add the supplementary remark, 'I mean—it's a fairly straightforward operation, isn't it?'

Jamie nodded. 'It is. You think that consultants should tackle only the tricky ops? Are we so aloof and inaccessible, then?'

'Don't put words into my mouth, Mr Brennan!' retorted Sarah crisply and saw Sister hide a smile. 'I wondered why you were doing it and not your registrar.'

He couldn't really tell her the truth, certainly not in front of Sister. That his registrar was becoming increasingly unreliable and stressed out and that he was going to have to have a long talk with him to find out why.

'My registrar is not as *au fait* with the procedure as I am,' he replied smoothly. 'And this lady has had a very distressing obstetric history. It took her many years to get pregnant in the first place and then she had three miscarriages in as many years. That is particularly hard for a woman to take. The last took place five years ago and the couple had rather given up hope of ever conceiving again— and certainly of carrying a healthy baby to term.

'Mrs Redwood is now thirty-eight. This might be her last chance of pregnancy—the only baby she might ever have. In other words it's an especially precious baby and that's why I shall be doing the operation myself. Does that satisfy you, Sarah?'

It did. Sarah thought how wonderful and fervent and passionate he had looked as he had answered her initial query. And how gladdened she had been by the fact that he was a caring, understanding and compassionate doctor. If only. . . If *only* he had not followed up his answer with that supplementary question of his own. Because his final aside concerning the subject of satisfaction was one that made her cheeks grow hot and pink. Had he said it on purpose just to embarrass her?

'Yes, thank you, Mr Brennan,' Sarah murmured quietly, her lashes falling in two sooty half-moons to conceal her eyes, not daring to meet that mocking, questioning gaze.

He found the way that she blushed quite enchanting but it stabbed troublesomely at his conscience. He found it hard to believe that such a beautiful young woman in her mid-twenties had still been a virgin but perhaps that was the way that young women were these days. It simply had not occurred to him that she might be and if he had known he almost certainly would have stopped.

Or would he? he asked himself with painful honesty. Would he have been able to stop himself? He had been in a sexual desert for so long and Sarah had been like warm, sweet water, bringing him to life again.

But he had been the one with the experience; he had been the one who should have tempered passion. And if Sarah was now pregnant then the blame, if blame could be apportioned in such circumstances, would rest at his feet.

The phone shrilled noisily on the desk and Sister moved to answer it, leaving Jamie alone with Sarah.

'Hi,' he said softly.

She wanted to melt; she wanted to say 'Hi' back to him in that curiously husky tone which so reminded her of the things that he had whispered to her in bed and which, she suspected, had been his intention.

But the fear of being hurt even more badly than she already had been kept her face calm and composed. 'I'd better do some work,' she said lightly and made to move away but Jamie stepped directly in her path so that she was forced to stop. And to look at him.

'Sarah,' he began, 'I want to explain—' But his bleeper began to shrill in his pocket.

Saved by the bell, thought Sarah with a mixture of relief and regret. 'I'll let you answer that,' she said.

'No! I need to talk to you.'

Sarah was aware of the interested eyes of a pupil midwife and knew from the set of Sister's shoulders that she was able to hear their conversation perfectly. She shook her head. 'We can't talk. Not here.'

'No. Not here. What time do you finish?'

Pride warred with her soft heart. She ought to tell him to go take a hike. She ought to make him wait at least a day. But his eyes were shadowed

and his face tense. And perhaps he had a good
reason for bedding her and then disappearing. 'I
finish at four-thirty,' she told him.

'And I'm operating this afternoon.' He frowned
as he mentally tried to work out what his commitments were. It was a long list, with a tricky case
tacked onto the end. A young woman not much
older than Sarah with a particularly virulent form
of cancer known as adenocarcinoma. He was going
to have to perform an extended hysterectomy. And
that could take time.

'It doesn't matter,' said Sarah quickly.

'Oh, but it does,' he contradicted, and his gaze
was straight and steady and serious. 'You know it
does. Can I see you later this evening?'

'What time?'

'I have to get Harriet settled.' If he read to her
he could leave Marianne to actually get her into
bed, which meant that they would have time to eat
together. 'Say about eight-thirty?'

Sarah nodded. 'OK, then. Eight-thirty it is.'

'Could we have supper somewhere? There's a
very good Italian restaurant just down the road.'

Sarah's first inclination was to refuse the supper
but then she thought about the most likely alterna-
tive. That Jamie would arrive at her flat and one
thing would lead to another and they'd end up in
bed together. And. . .

She knew that it was a little late in the day for
prudence but it was somehow vitally important to
her that he did not just categorise her as someone
who was 'easy'. And at least his invitation to

supper sounded like a proper date and not a repeat of their last, rather illicit, liaison.

She nodded her head, allowing herself the smallest smile. 'Thank you,' she answered formally. 'I'd like that. And now, if you'll excuse me, I really have work to do.'

'See you later,' he murmured. He watched her retreating back as she made her way gracefully down the ward and had to stifle a small groan of lust at the sight of all those heavenly soft curves and the way that the blue uniform clung to the neat line of her bottom. And he remembered that bottom bare.

Jamie felt tiny beads of sweat break out on his forehead, felt his pulse rocket and his breathing become shallow.

Oh, Lord, how he wanted her!

CHAPTER SIX

THANKFULLY the rest of Sarah's day was frantically busy and so she was able to successfully put
all thoughts of Jamie Brennan on hold.

To her delight Sister asked her to take charge
of a woman who was being admitted to the labour
ward. It was a straightforward, though protracted,
labour and an hour after Sarah was supposed to
have been off duty she was still there, gently
encouraging the woman in her breathing and
taking turns with the husband to comfortingly rub
the small of the woman's back.

Sister came in at five-thirty. 'How are we
doing?' she asked Sarah.

'Everything has been going smoothly,'
answered Sarah, 'and Mrs O'Donnell is eight
centimetres dilated.'

'Hmm,' observed Sister, as she cast an experienced eye over the woman. 'This could still take
some time. First baby and all that. Do you want
to go off duty now, Sarah? Let one of the afternoon
staff take over?'

Sarah saw the disappointment written on the
woman's face, a disappointment that she felt
keenly, too. During childbirth the relationship
between mother and midwife was very close and
very intense and most women preferred the same

midwife to stay with them throughout their labour. The midwife preferred it, too. Professionally and emotionally it was very frustrating to have assisted from the very beginning and then miss out on the best bit of all—seeing the birth of a baby!

'I'll stay for a bit longer—if you don't mind, Sister?'

Sister smiled broadly. 'Mind? Why on earth should I mind? Stay as long as you like, Sarah!'

A baby girl was dutifully delivered half an hour later and Sarah had her photo taken with mother and baby and accepted a glass of champagne from the proud father.

But it was almost six-thirty when she arrived back at her room and changed from her uniform into jeans and a T-shirt in double-quick time. Whatever else she did—supper date or no supper date—she simply *had* to go shopping. She still had absolutely nothing in her kitchen bar half a bottle of sherry. . .

One of the other nurses from the block had told her where to go for provisions and she found the shop quite easily. It was quite a walk there and back but she felt much better afterwards for the fresh air and exercise.

She lugged her carrier bags into the small kitchen and unpacked fruit and vegetables, butter, cheese, ham, bread, coffee, tea, biscuits and yoghurt. She had also bought rice and pasta and a couple of jars of tomato sauce for her store cupboard. Just in case. . .

In case of what? she asked herself mockingly.

In case Jamie Brennan starts popping in regularly for one of your home-cooked meals?

And only respect for other people's property stopped her from slamming the fridge door shut after putting the last of her shopping away!

The room still looked unlived-in. It was not really the impression that she liked giving. She had not unpacked half the little photos and ornaments that she had brought with her from home but it was getting on for eight o'clock and she would not have time tonight. Not if she wanted to put some effort into getting ready. So that she looked her absolute best.

And she did.

It was partly pride—because she had been dressed in faded denim and had looked so tatty the other night. And it was partly to make him instantly desire her. So that she could hold him at arm's length and show him that, yes, she *could* show a little self-restraint.

She found some bubble bath and ran herself a deep tub, and the warm water and the scented steam which filled the bathroom relaxed her. She washed her hair, too, and spent far longer than usual drying it strand by strand with the hair drier.

Supper in Southbury with her new consultant. Who was also her lover, she reminded herself. That was, of course, assuming that he still wanted to be. And that *she* still wanted him to be.

And she did!

So what should she wear? What was the Italian restaurant like? She didn't want to look too dressed up but, there again, she did not want to look too casual either!

In the end she opted for a silk, long-sleeved shirt in her favourite green—this time a dark forest green. She wore it tucked into a pair of black, tapered trousers. She made her face up with care and put on her favourite dangly jade earrings, which Benedict and Verity had brought her back from China when they had gone on their much-belated honeymoon. Then she made herself a cup of coffee and ate a plain biscuit with it because she was absolutely ravenous, took her cup and sat down beside the window and pretended to flick through a magazine while she waited.

Jamie's list had gone on for much longer than he, even in his most pessimistic of projections, could have anticipated. But at least he had managed to contact Marianne earlier in the day.

'Can you babysit tonight?' he had asked.

Marianne hesitated. 'It's very short notice—'

'I know. I'm sorry. It's just that something rather important has come up.'

'A date?' queried Marianne in surprise.

'Hmm, yes. I don't ask very often, do I?' He put on his most pleading voice and heard her sigh on the other end of the phone.

'I'm waiting for a phonecall myself,' Marianne explained. 'Tell you what—if he doesn't call I'll babysit. If he *does* I'll only accept if I can find a replacement. How's that?'

'You are a marvel, Marianne,' he said fervently.

'I don't know what I'm going to do without you.' Which was true. When his daughter's nanny went up to university in the autumn he would be left in the lurch.

He ploughed his way through his afternoon list but his last case—the young woman with adenocarcinoma requiring an extended hysterectomy—was very time-consuming, partly due to the fact that the patient was obese. It was a relatively long procedure at the best of times but obesity made the mechanics of the operation even longer. Excess fat made organs inaccessible, as well as increasing the risk of anaesthetic complications.

He had just been finishing when A and E had rung up. They had a young woman with a suspected ectopic pregnancy—the medical name for any pregnancy developing outside the cavity of the uterus. As well as the potential of life-threatening haemmorhage, ectopic pregnancy also carried with it the likelihood of impaired fertility. Action simply could not be delayed.

'Send her up, then,' barked Jamie. He flicked a quick glance at the clock and his mouth tightened behind the paper mask he wore. 'And let's get some blood cross-matched as soon as possible, can we, Sister?'

All hell broke loose when the trolley was rushed up from A and E since by now the patient was in profound shock.

'Has she had any morphia?' demanded Jamie.

The theatre sister had snatched the notes from

the trolley and was scanning through them. 'Nothing yet.'

'Right. Let's draw some up quickly. We'll combat the shock and restore the blood volume—then we'll do a laparotomy.'

It was tense and it was messy, with bright blood everywhere, and it wasn't until Jamie had located the problem that he began to feel more confident. Once you knew where the problem lay you could go about finding a solution to it. In surgery the most dangerous thing was ignorance, he always thought.

'I'm going to have to perform a salpingectomy,' he said hurriedly, as he peered down the laparoscope with a frown. Sometimes the Fallopian tube could be saved but not in this case. The pregnancy had indeed badly ruptured the tube itself and he would need to remove it, thus slightly limiting the woman's chances of conceiving again. An added complication was that once a woman had had an ectopic pregnancy she was much more likely to have another.

However, once Jamie had clamped the bleeding tube and stopped the flow of blood he was able to breathe more easily as he proceeded with the operation and the woman's condition improved quite dramatically.

He was smiling as he pulled off his latex gloves and hurled them into the bin with a show-off shot. Satisfaction washed over him. A successful emergency operation to conclude a busy day and the prospect of a date with a beautiful woman who. . .

Jamie blanched, the smile dying on his face as he saw the clock-face. Blast and blast! It was almost eight-fifteen!

If he had been a single man there would have been no problem. He could have changed in Theatres after his shower because he always kept a spare set of clothes there. Sometimes, thankfully rarely, he had been unable to leave the hospital for the entire weekend and had been glad of the opportunity to put fresh garments on.

But he was not a single man, he reminded himself as he drove home in the bright red Jag, resisting the temptation to break the speed limit in the magnificently powerful car.

He was not a married man either. There was no wife to nag him; to berate him for being late.

Just a daughter!

Harriet had obviously been listening out for him, since she pulled the front door open as soon as the car slid to a halt on the gravelled drive. She was still, he noted impatiently, in her school uniform and not all bathed and ready for bed as he might have hoped. And Blue, her dog—who was yapping beside her feet—looked as though he had just been given a mud-bath.

'So there you are!' were her opening, accusing words and she glowered.

'Hello, Harriet,' said Jamie, trying to keep the weariness from out of his voice. 'Had a good day, darling?'

'Marianne says you're going out tonight and

that she can't babysit!' said his daughter pugnaciously.

On cue Marianne appeared at the door, looking unusually smart. Her hair looked suspiciously damp at the edges and about twice its usual volume and the ubiquitous jeans and T-shirt had been abandoned in favour of an ankle-length white dress, which was smart if rather creased.

'Hi, Jamie!' said Marianne, rather uncertainly. 'Harriet, could you go and turn the tap off in the bath?'

Harriet hesitated for a moment before running off, her face still sulky, and Jamie knew that the battle had not been abandoned but merely postponed.

'So he rang?' he queried of Marianne, who still stood on the doorstep.

'Mmm. Got a date. Sorry. Mrs Marshall from across the road said she can be here in minutes.'

Jamie pushed down his instinctive feeling of disappointment. Mrs Marshall had a heart of gold but she was in her late sixties and was not at all keen on Harriet's dog, who at that moment jumped up at Jamie and left a pattern of muddy paw-prints all over his cream trousers.

'Get *down*, Blue!' he shouted, and Blue made a gruff sound in the back of his throat and loped off round the side of the house, leaving Jamie to hope that none of the back doors was open or the pale carpet was going to take a hammering!

'All the doors are shut,' said Marianne instantly, as if reading his mind, only emphasing how different she was in attitude to Mrs Marshall.

Mrs Marshall was also a stickler for routine, which Jamie did not think was a bad thing but Harriet *did*. He felt like pleading with Marianne not to let him down. Not tonight, of all nights. But she had been the most fabulously reliable person, especially for an eighteen-year-old. And she was great with Harriet.

'You look fantastic,' he told her.

'Do I?'

'Yeah. The dress could do with a bit of an iron, though.'

Marianne stared at him in disbelief, the generation gulf between them glaringly obvious. 'Jamie!' she chided. 'It's linen! It's *supposed* to look like that!'

'Oh,' he said, affecting a somewhat mystified voice, and Marianne saw the twinkle in his eyes and burst out laughing.

'Very funny!' she giggled.

'Go on,' he told her. 'You'd better get going. Before I change my mind and beg you to stay!'

'*Thanks*, Jamie!'

'So, who's the date?'

She rubbed the toe of her white shoe self-consciously against the marble of the step. 'Oh, no one, really,' she lied outrageously. 'Medical student on Dad's firm.'

'Oh, dear,' Jamie said, rather solemnly. 'You aren't going to marry a doctor, are you?'

Marianne's head jerked up at his question, her expression of horror almost comic. 'No way! Do you think I'm nuts?' she answered fervently, then grinned. 'No, on second thoughts, don't answer that! 'Night, Jamie. See you in the morning.'

Jamie stood watching her as she let herself out of the front gate, his lips curved into a wry smile as he thought how ironic it was. The public had this fixation with the idea of medics being so eligible and yet anyone who had any dealings with doctors knew that the hours and the stresses and demands of the job put more strain on relationships than most professions.

Still, there was no time for philosophising now. '*Harriet*!' he called at the top of his voice.

'Daddy! Daddy! Quickly! Blue's just been sick—all over the *carpet*!'

It was after nine before the carpet was cleaned to Mrs Marshall's satisfaction and by then Jamie had to go and take another shower. He was late enough as it was but it was hardly going to endear him to Sarah further if he turned up smelling of dog-sick!

He tried ringing her but to no avail. It seemed that there were no telephones in the nurses' rooms.

'Isn't there one in the corridor?' he asked the operator in desperation.

'It's out of order at the moment,' she replied triumphantly. 'People kept stealing the money!'

'But not the nurses, surely?' Jamie said defensively.

'No one knows *who* it was!' deflected the operator with gloomy satisfaction.

It was getting on for ten when he finally knocked

on Sarah's door and although he could see light spilling from the room onto the landing corridor no one answered the door.

This was, most emphatically, *not* his day.

'Sarah,' he began tiredly. 'Please open up. I know you're in there!'

'Then you must also know that I have no intention of answering the door!' came a muffled-sounding voice from behind the door.

'Then I'll just have to stay here all night!'

'Do that!' she retorted sharply. 'In fact—do what you damned well like!'

For half a second he wondered if it was all worth this hassle. Maybe celibacy *was* easier. But then he remembered how it had felt to have her in his arms, lying next to him. And not just the act of making love, though that had been sublime in itself. More than that, it had been the closeness between them. The communion of lying together, their passion spent, strangely united against the world.

'Sarah, *please*! Just give me two minutes, won't you? I can explain everything.'

There was a pause while he waited, praying that she would open the door.

Sarah sat on the bed, all hunched up, her arms wrapped protectively around her knees. She was sorely tempted to tell him where to go. She couldn't *believe* that his behaviour could be this atrocious.

And that was the whole point, surely.

She hardly knew him—well, OK—she knew

him in the biblical sense, better than she had known any other man. But. . . And it was a *big* but. . .

From what little she did know of him, she found it impossible to believe that he would have deliberately been as late as this. Not when he had been so eager to see her again.

She pulled the door open.

Jamie was so relieved that she *had* given in and opened the door that he said the first thing which came into his head. And then worried that it sounded dutiful rather than admiring. 'You look lovely.' She did, too—with her hair all newly washed again and she was wearing some gorgeous white nightshirt thing that swept down almost to the floor, leaving only the most tantalising glimpse of a shapely ankle showing. It was, he was to quickly discover, entirely the wrong thing to say.

'No, I don't!' she snapped back.

'You—don't?'

'I *did* look nice! In the outfit I was wearing almost *two hours ago*!' She fixed him with an accusingly sizzling emerald stare.

'I can explain—'

'It's much too late for explanations,' said Sarah frostily.

There was only one thing for it.

He didn't want to be done for breaking and entering so his arm snaked in through the door to grab hold of her arm and do what he had been wanting to do all day.

Sarah found herself being pulled out of her room

and hauled up against his hard, lean body and she stared up at him in surprise.

And something in that startled, almost vulnerable, look stirred Jamie far more than lust and he sought her lips with a hunger which eclipsed even Saturday night—a strange, emotional kind of hunger that he had never thought he would feel again.

Sarah swayed, succumbed to the expert way his mouth moved over hers and felt her body respond hotly and meltingly into that powerful embrace. Desire filled her like a gift from heaven and yet disappointment tainted it.

So this was what it was going to be, she thought, and although his mouth tasted just as sweet as it kissed her so thoroughly and so passionately her heart sank as she anticipated what would follow.

An affair, that's what. Of the most sordid type. She would be squeezed in around his work, his daughter and his other life. No deliciously slow exploration, the kind of mature relationship she had always dreamed of finding. Instead, she was to be hidden away in her room for the occasional liaison like this. Kept secret from the world like some shameful addiction.

Unless she had the strength of mind to resist him. . .

Through the swamping mists of desire Jamie sensed her mental, if not her physical, withdrawal. For she remained as soft and as pliant and as responsive as when he had first begun to kiss her. And he could feel the heated swell of her breasts beneath the flimsy wrap she wore. Whatever she might be feeling there was no doubt that she wanted him. And he was experienced enough in the ways of love to know that it would not be difficult to have her naked and compliant in his arms again within minutes.

But Jamie did not want her on those terms. Let's face it, he thought. He could have had sex with lots of different women if he had so chosen. But he had not. It had to be something special. *With* someone special. Which Sarah was.

He stopped kissing her and she stared up at him, a vague disquiet on her face mixed with the hectic flush of arrested passion.

'Come on,' he said, and gently pushed her into the room and Sarah felt like a sacrificial lamb about to be led to the ceremonial bed.

The question was whether or not she was going to allow herself to be treated like an emotional victim.

No! She most certainly was not. With determination she pulled back her strong, square shoulders, quite unprepared for the almost despairing look on Jamie's face as she did so until she realised that the movement revealed the deep cleft between her breasts.

'Go and get dressed!' he growled.

It was so exactly the opposite of what she had imagined he might want from her that Sarah blinked at him in bemusement. 'W-what?' she questioned, in confusion.

The inherent innocence of her query only

increased his guilt at what he had allowed to happen on Saturday night. 'Go and get dressed,' he repeated rather desperately. 'Please, Sarah. Before I change my mind.'

Her clear green eyes were candid. 'Why?'

'We're supposed to be having supper, aren't we?'

'Well, we were. But it's—'

'I know,' he interrupted with a small smile. 'It's late. And it'll be even later the longer we stand talking about it and lessen our chances still further of finding a table at this time of night. Besides which—' and his thick lashes shuttered the dazzling blue eyes '—if you don't change out of that thing you're wearing then you may have to go hungry. For food, anyway,' he finished with a smile and was rewarded with a blush.

She scuttled into the bedroom rather self-consciously, hastily shutting the door behind her, though in view of what had happened between them before it seemed a rather pointless act of modesty! She was too dazed and too excited to give much thought to what to wear, especially since her discarded outfit was lying in a crumpled heap next to the wall at which she had thrown it! Instead, she put on what she always wore in moments of crisis—though this seemed the worst crisis of her life to date!

Her little black dress.

It was short and beautifully cut and utterly classic. The scoop neck transformed her neck and cleavage into a heavenly vision and the line of the dress did wonders for her waist and hips and bottom.

She slipped her feet into neat, patent-leather pumps and picked up a matching clutch-bag but didn't bother applying any more make-up, just raked a brush through the thick, dark silk of her wavy hair until she had it in some sort of order and it spilt with studied disarray all over her shoulders.

When she went back into the sitting room, however, she revelled in the long, hard look of approbation he gave her and felt her confidence grow to something approaching its normal proportions.

'Wow!' he said softly. 'You look wonderful.'

'But you said I looked wonderful when you first came in.' She raised her eyebrows pertly.

'Different kind of wonderful,' he answered huskily, thinking that if he did not get out of here very soon then all his good intentions would be lost to the world. 'Let's go,' he ordered abruptly.

Sarah couldn't think of a thing to say to him as they walked along the corridor of the nurses' home but that was partly due to the fact that several nurses gave them some very curious stares as they passed by. And Jamie himself seemed deep in thought as they reached the car park and he began heading towards a pillar-box red Jaguar.

Sarah made a disbelieving little sound as she saw the sleek-looking machine and Jamie heard it and smiled.

'Surprised?' he murmured, with a dazzling blue sideways glance.

He was a widower with a child. A fairly prosperous consultant. Perhaps she had imagined him driving something more solid and sedate than this. She looked at the low, definitely sexy car and then at Jamie and smiled back at him. 'No, not really. It suits you.'

'Then let's go and eat.'

He drove to the Italian restaurant he had originally planned to take her to.

'Though they may have given our table away,' he explained.

The restaurant was small and intimate and the food was excellent.

And the waiter, it seemed, knew Jamie.

'Mr Brennan!' he exclaimed loudly. 'You don't remember me?'

Jamie studied him for a moment, concentrating fiercely, then shook his head. 'I'm sorry,' he said, 'but I don't.'

'But I know *you*!' laughed the waiter. 'You the very best baby doctor here in Southbury!'

It transpired that Jamie had delivered the man's son just after he had arrived at the hospital to take up his post.

'I can't believe this!' giggled Sarah delightedly as the waiter insisted on going off to fetch them a complimentary bottle of wine. 'This is a set-up! He's your stooge, isn't he? He must be! And whenever you take a girl out you prime him to pretend that you're the world's best doctor!'

'You've found me out,' he sighed mockingly. 'You're much, *much* too perceptive, Sarah!'

Soon the table was festooned with photos of the baby Luciano and Sarah's stomach had just begun to rumble protestingly when the manager came over to rescue them, scooping up the photos and handing them back to the waiter before sending him away to get them each a menu. 'Otherwise they won't eat!' he complained. 'And this doctor, he needs to keep his strength up!'

And Sarah didn't dare meet Jamie's eyes.

They ordered Parma ham with melon, followed by a mushroom risotto, and sat sipping the superb Bardolino while napkins were unfolded and delicious warm bread rolls were placed in the middle of the table. And it wasn't until they had been left alone that Jamie reached over the table and laid his strong brown hand over hers.

'I owe you an apology,' he said softly.

'For being late?'

'That, too. But also for the other night.'

Sarah stopped crumbling a piece of bread and looked up, her green eyes suddenly very big in her white, shocked face. 'Why?' she whispered.

But then the waiter reappeared, carrying their first courses, and Jamie knew that this was the wrong time and the wrong place to attempt to put his thoughts into words. He shook his dark head.

'I'll tell you later,' he promised. 'Eat your supper before it gets cold.'

Half of her was relieved to get off the awkward subject of Saturday night. 'But it *is* cold!'

'Ah!' He affected a look of confusion. 'Better eat it anyway, then!'

He told her why he had been late—the over-long operating list and Harriet's dog being ill.

Sarah adored animals and immediately put her fork down. 'Is she all right?'

'Who, Harriet?' he enquired, deadpan.

He had a very irreverent sense of humour, Sarah decided. Even worse than her brother's—and that was saying something! 'No. The dog.'

'Oh, the dog!' Jamie shrugged. 'Yeah, Blue's all right. I explained to Harriet that if you feed dogs disproportionately large amounts of chocolate then it doesn't exactly do them a lot of good!'

He did not mention to Sarah that the thought had crossed his mind that it had been a deliberate act of sabotage on Harriet's part. She was not stupid; she knew a lot about dogs. And she had *never* given Blue that much chocolate before. Strange that she should choose to do so on the very night that her father was venturing out on his first 'date' since her mother had died.

And once more guilt reached out to stab at his heart.

Sarah saw the disconcerted look which crossed his face. 'Does Harriet mind you being here with me tonight?' she asked perceptively.

He put his fork down and pushed his plate away with a sigh. 'I don't know,' he admitted honestly. 'I haven't asked her.'

'But, given a choice?'

He looked at her in surprise, amazed that she wanted to pursue such a potentially difficult subject so early on. Particularly when some of the answers she might receive might not be the ones she wanted to hear. . .

'Given a choice, she would obviously prefer me to be at home with her.' He paused, perhaps to give Sarah an inkling of what might lie in store should the relationship flourish. 'She's been playing up a little bit.'

His honesty completely disarmed her and Sarah began to butter another piece of bread. 'And does she play up for all your girlfriends?' she queried softly.

Jamie hesitated. Was now the right time to tell her that she was the first one? Because you couldn't really count Verity. Verity had just been a friend, even though at the time he had wanted so much more than friendship. As he opened his mouth to speak the waiter whipped their plates away and he was secretly relieved that he could change the subject.

He could see already that his position was loaded—he was going into this relationship with so much more baggage than a single man. It was bound to be heavy at times. So why not forget potential problems on this, their first, date and just enjoy the occasion for what it was?

So they played the dating game.

Jamie found that the barely remembered rules soon came back to him—of finding common interests, of listening rather than speaking all the time and, very importantly, of making her laugh. And he seemed, he noticed with immense pleasure, rather good at making her laugh.

As for Sarah she was simply aware of having the best time of her life, falling more and more deeply for the handsome and witty man across the table as the evening wore on. In fact, when he started talking in an impassioned way about his research Sarah was so fascinated that by the end of the evening she realised that she hadn't mentioned her family once. And for Sarah, baby of the family, that was some record!

The only slight disappointment was that she had not lost her normal healthy appetite since, by the end of the evening, she was convinced that she was on the brink of falling in love and people on the brink of falling in love were supposed to be disinterested in food, weren't they? She spooned up the last of Jamie's zabaglione and found him watching her intently.

'I eat too much,' she grimaced as she licked the creamy, Marsala-whipped concoction from her lips.

He seemed utterly riveted by the movement. 'Nonsense,' he murmured. 'You've got a beautiful body.'

They stared at one another in silence and the restaurant might not have existed for all the notice they took of the comings and goings around them.

Jamie cleared his throat. 'Would you like some coffee?'

Dizzy with anticipation, Sarah shook her head. 'N-no, thanks,' she stumbled, suddenly shy.

'Then shall we go?'

'OK.'

The drive back was almost as tense as the outward journey. Sarah stared fixedly out of the window but even the distant glimmer of the moonlight on the tar-dark sea failed to catch her attention for more than a moment.

Jamie drew into the car park and switched off the engine. 'I'll walk you to your room,' he said, and his voice was so expressionless that Sarah had no idea what he was thinking.

And he did not take her arm either so that Sarah was bewildered. She had thought that they had been close in the restaurant, exceptionally close. And yet now he was walking beside her like a stranger, his head bent and his hands thrust deep into the pockets of his trousers.

Perhaps . . . , she thought, stricken. Perhaps she had misread the signs. Perhaps he was regretting asking her out; regretting going to bed with her. Maybe he was working out a polite way to let her down.

Well, he needn't bother, Sarah thought proudly. She was not desperate enough to have to crawl and beg the man!

It seemed to take for ever to reach her door and when she slid the key into the lock she turned to him with a polite little smile.

'Thank you very much for a lovely evening,' she said stiffly.

Jamie frowned. He had felt her retreat from him. The warm, laughing woman that he had shared such an enjoyable evening with had become all cold and frosty once they had left the restaurant.

'It doesn't have to be over yet, does it?' he asked softly.

She had been a walk-over once; she did not intend repeating the experience. She stifled a yawn. 'I rather think it does. I'm on early in the morning—'

'Sarah,' he interrupted urgently, 'are we going to carry on making polite little chit-chat like Saturday night never happened?'

His candid words shattered the barrier that she had been trying to erect between them and removed her own inhibitions. 'What do you want?'

'I'd like to come in and talk to you.'

'Really?' She gave a laugh which, even to her own ears, sounded harsh and cynical. 'Is that all you want to do?'

He half pushed her through the door and pulled it violently shut behind him before turning to her, his face furious at the intended slur in her words. 'No!' he answered savagely. 'That is *not* all that I want to do. In fact, talking is the last thing I'm thinking about right at this moment! What I would *like* to do, Sarah, is to take all the time in the world to show you just how properly exquisite and satisfying love-making *can* be.'

'B-but it *was*,' she answered in confusion as she remembered the closeness, the melding together of their bodies and the incredible sense of being as one. 'Wasn't it?'

'No,' he answered gently. 'Not for you. Not properly. But it was your first time. Darling, please don't turn away like that. What is it?'

She kept her face averted. 'It's *you*!' she blurted out. 'Talking about it like that!'

'Like what? Aren't we allowed to talk about it? Do you just want to turn the light out and do it?' he stormed, and wondered if he had gone too far when he heard her shocked inrush of breath.

Sarah's heart had started pounding furiously. She seemed to have dived headlong into an adult world with little or no preparation. She sat down on the settee and stared up at him and his face softened.

'That's better,' he said, coming to sit beside her and lifting her chin to plant a soft, sweet kiss on her mouth.

Sarah relaxed into the ease of that kiss immediately but Jamie pulled away. He could not run away from the possible repercussions of their love-making.

'You could be pregnant,' he said heavily.

It was something that she had been trying desperately hard not to think about. She was certainly worried about it and yet she wondered if she should feel more horrified about it than she actually did. 'Yes.'

'Is it a possibility?'

Sarah swallowed. 'Yes.'

He sighed and then kissed her again but for much longer than before and when he stopped kissing her he looked directly into her eyes with a soft tenderness which thrilled her in spite of all her fears and misgivings. 'When will you know?'

Still weak from that kiss, Sarah was able to

discuss it almost as matter-of-factly. 'In about a week or so.'

'Then we'll cross that bridge if and when we come to it.' He noted that there was a sort of slumberous, dreamy quality about her, a smile playing at the corners of those full, luscious lips. Pregnancy would suit her, he thought with a sudden protectiveness and leaned over to take her in his arms.

'It's past midnight,' he told her reluctantly, 'and I have to go.'

'B-but I thought you had a nanny?'

'I do. But she doesn't live in. She just stays over whenever I'm on call or when she *is* babysitting— which she isn't tonight because she has a date. Tonight the formidable Mrs Marshall is ensconced in my house. She will have obsessively straightened every cushion and pillow in the house and she will have washed all Harriet's school clothes by hand since she doesn't believe in washing machines! She will also,' he concluded softly, 'be raring to get home to Mr Marshall and I will already have earned the famous Marshall look of disapproval.'

He stroked his hand down the side of her face. 'I want to make love to you more than words can say, Sarah,' he told her softly. 'But there isn't time to do you justice,' he added on a wicked murmur.

'Oh, this is hopeless,' said Sarah brutally.

He shook his head. 'Not hopeless. Just difficult. Tell you what—I'm not on call at the weekend. Would you like to spend the day with us?'

'Us?'

'Mmm.' Jamie observed her watchfully. He came as a package, after all, so she might as well see what she was letting herself in for. 'With me and Harriet.'

She read the challenge in his eyes. 'What's this?' she quizzed. 'Trial by ordeal?'

Jamie laughed, pleased that she wasn't afraid to voice her scepticism. 'Perhaps a baptism of fire might be a more accurate way of describing it,' he observed wryly. 'But I have to tell you that underneath her sometimes prickly manner Harriet is an absolute darling.'

'I bet she is,' smiled Sarah, with genuine belief. 'It's perfectly natural for her to feel jealous.'

His blue eyes crinkled at the corners. 'So,' he probed gently. 'Is that a date? Say, next Saturday?'

She wished that he wasn't going. And in her heart of hearts she wished that she wasn't going to face such a crucial test as meeting his daughter so early on. Still, Sarah had not been head girl of her prestigious girls' school through ducking a challenge, however unwelcome. Besides, she had already met Harriet. And liked her. And Harriet seemed to have liked her, too. But that was before either of them had connected the other to Jamie.

'Saturday sounds great,' she told him.

CHAPTER SEVEN

JAMIE drove home as frustration and longing transmuted themselves into a desire for danger and it wasn't until he heard the distant shriek of a siren and saw the sickly blue light of the police car in his rear mirror that he realised that he had been speeding.

He pulled over and wound the window down to see the stern face of the policeman as he walked over towards the Jag, a resigned expression on his face.

'Evening, sir,' he began, in the time-honoured way. 'This your car, is it?'

Jamie felt stupid. And furious with himself. He had not been going especially fast but he had been *just* over the speed limit.

He suspected that if he had not been a doctor pleading fatigue as an excuse for a momentary lapse he would have had his licence endorsed. As it was he was grateful that at least he had drunk only one glass of wine over the whole evening and the policeman hadn't even bothered to breathalyse him. Just told him in a rather resigned voice not to do it again.

This all took time and when he arrived home it was to see lights blazing from all parts of the house and alarm ate into his heart as he rushed inside to find Mrs Marshall in the sitting room, a reproachful look on her face as she pointedly looked down at a puffy-faced Harriet who was half-asleep on her lap.

'What's going on?' demanded Jamie urgently.

At the sound of her father's voice Harriet woke up and began snuffling.

He was beside her in seconds. 'What's happened, sweetheart?' he urged and then, in a calmer voice because he could see that she was all in one piece, 'What's going on, Mrs Marshall?'

'It's Blue!' put in Harriet, sniffing. 'She was sick again—we had to call the vet out!' Her lips trembled and her brown eyes filled with accusing tears. 'We tried bleeping you but the hospital said you weren't answering!'

Jamie nodded, his analytical brain immediately shifting her accusations into order of priority. 'How's Blue now?'

'Sleeping,' sniffed Harriet. 'The vet gave her an injection and is calling again tomorrow.'

'Good.' He said his next words very slowly and deliberately because he thought that Mrs Marshall should hear them, too. 'Listen, Harriet, I'm sorry you couldn't contact me. I wasn't answering my bleeper because I wasn't on call. I only take it with me when I *am* on call—that's what the bleeper is for. I went out for dinner and I was quite happy to leave you in Mrs Marshall's care. Other families don't get bleeped when they go out for dinner, now do they?'

'Other families have mummies!' said Harriet

bitterly, and tears began to slide down her cheeks again.

It was three o'clock by the time he had got her settled and then the dog was sick again. Jamie contemplated calling the vet out on a second visit but Blue seemed a bit better so in the end he hauled the basket and the dog up the stairs as carefully as he could and broke a lifetime's rule of banning animals from bedrooms by putting Blue's basket at the foot of his bed.

Sarah had a lovely morning at work the following day. She walked into the office to be told by Sister, 'There's a labour just started in cubicle four. One of the night staff is in with her now. A Mrs Delia Herley. It's a second baby and her husband is there with her. If you'd like to go down she'll hand over to you and you can take over.'

'Right,' said Sarah, pleased to have the excitement of a baby to deliver because that was, after all, what she liked doing most. But she was also rather relieved not to be accompanying Sister on Jamie's ward round, which she knew was due in about an hour. Not after that frank discussion they had had last night.

What if she *was* pregnant?

As she walked towards cubicle four she found that she had pressed the palm of her hand experimentally over her stomach and then pulled it away as she realised just what she was doing! As if she could tell from the feel of her belly after a couple of days! And her a midwife, too!

She smiled at the thought and then drew herself

up sharply, her heart beating very fast as she acknowledged how readily she had come to terms with the possibility of having Jamie's baby.

More than come to terms with it, in fact. The thought made her want to shiver—partly through fear but mostly, yes, mostly with excitement. And women usually only wanted to carry a man's baby for one reason alone.

Am I falling in love with Jamie Brennan? she asked herself. Can you love someone you barely know? Poets believed that you could. And their relationship, if you could call it that, seemed to have been very intense right from the word go. If it *wasn't* love it felt like something pretty darned close to it!

Resolutely she put the thought out of her mind as she pushed the door of cubicle four open to find her patient on all fours on the bed. Sarah smiled, loving the fact that maternity care had moved with the times. These days a woman could probably successfully argue her case for having her baby whilst swinging from a chandelier!

It was hot in the room and the woman's thick blonde curls were falling all over her face. A tall man standing beside her looked up rather helplessly as Sarah entered the room.

'Hello, Delia,' said Sarah immediately, giving the woman a bright and, she hoped, efficient smile. 'My name is Sarah Jackson,' she added chattily, since it was terribly important to establish a rapport with the labouring mother straight away. 'And I've come to take over from the midwife who has been looking after you during the night.'

The midwife, whose black-circled eyes advertised the fact that it was her last night on duty, gave an abstracted nod as she scribbled something down on a chart.

Sarah walked over. 'Hi! How's it going? How's she getting on?'

The night nurse smiled as she put the chart down. 'Oh, really good! She's coping beautifully with the contractions. The baby is in a great position and the head is right down. All in all there are no problems.'

'When did you last examine her?'

'Just under three hours ago and she was about six centimetres dilated.' The night nurse glanced up at the clock. 'Oh, well, that's me finished. Better go—my kids will be waiting for me to take them to school! Bye, Delia, hope it all goes well!'

The labour was a classic one and might have come straight from one of the textbooks that Sarah had pored over during her midwifery training. She and Delia chatted inconsequentially and then Sarah checked her blood pressure and listened to the baby's heartbeat using the old-fashioned foetal ear-trumpet.

'How's she doing?' asked Delia quickly.

'Just fine,' smiled Sarah. 'Absolutely fine. Do you know that your baby is a girl, then?'

Delia shook her head so that her blonde curls waggled. 'No way! When I had the scan they asked me if I wanted to know the baby's sex but I said no, thanks! Imagine going through a long labour and not even having a surprise at the end! No, the reason I said ''she'' is that ever since I first got pregnant Johnny and I have been calling her Harriet—'

'Oh, that's the name of—' butted in Sarah eagerly, then halted as she saw Delia's interested expression.

'The name of who?' queried Delia.

'Er—the name of a friend's daughter,' answered Sarah weakly, and then could have kicked herself. If there was a possibility that you were pregnant by a man you were certainly entitled to call him your boyfriend!

Delia was laughing and joking between contractions but gradually her mood became more fractious as the strength of her contractions became stronger.

She was sweating profusely in the baggy T-shirt she wore and her blonde hair was falling in damp tendrils all around her face. She had been walking restlessly around the room, pausing only to stop for contractions, but suddenly she climbed laboriously back up onto the bed again and her husband immediately began rubbing her back.

'Leave me alone!' Delia beseeched loudly. 'For heaven's sake, Johnny, can't you just *leave me alone*!'

Johnny looked shocked and he stared at Sarah in confusion. 'But at the classes they told me to make sure I rubbed the small of my wife's back! It's all changed since we had our last baby,' he added rather plaintively.

'I think that perhaps that's an adaptable rule,' murmured Sarah diplomatically. 'The back-rubbing, I mean. Some women, in fact, find it immensely irritating.' Some women also became either very cross or very despairing as their labour progressed into its final stages, she thought as she watched Delia glaring at her husband.

'Why don't we take this big T-shirt off?' suggested Sarah gently.

'But it's one of mine!' protested Delia's husband. 'And in our classes they told us that the woman would probably feel much better if she wasn't wearing some constricting hospital gown which made her feel as though she was sick instead of participating in a perfectly normal act of nature!'

Sarah kept her smile. Some of the childbirth classes the women attended seemed to be actively *anti*-hospital and whilst she herself thought that interventionist techniques should be avoided wherever possible she also thought that every single birth was different and should be adapted to accordingly. 'We have some much cooler cotton gowns,' she coaxed softly. 'Why don't you try one, Delia? And maybe we could tie your hair back while we're at it—you'd be much more comfortable.'

Minutes later Delia was lying relaxed and more at ease on the bed, though absolutely exhausted by her last contraction. 'I want to push!' she panted desperately.

Sarah looked closely. She could see the perineum bulging and a tuft of what looked like ginger hair. Yep! This baby looked as though it was ready to make its entrance into the world! 'Try pushing at the next contraction, Delia,' she said and, to her delight, saw the baby's head coming down nicely. She pressed the buzzer for assistance. 'Baby's on the way!' she announced as she opened up her delivery pack and poured lotions and potions into the bowls. Then she put her gown and gloves on and swabbed the patient down.

There! The head was out. Sarah heard the door of the room open and close and someone walk into the room as she checked that the cord was not wrapped around the baby's head. Good! Assistance had arrived. It was not always possible to have another member of staff in the room during the delivery itself but it was preferable just in case anything went wrong.

Sarah delivered the anterior shoulder, pulling up the posterior shoulder so that the whole body could slip out, and then she delivered the baby itself onto the mother's stomach, saying exultantly, 'It *is* a girl!'

'Another one!' murmured Delia. 'Hello, Harriet!' and she smiled with tired delight as the proud father bent to put his arm around his wife and promptly burst into tears!

'Congratulations!' came a deep and delectably familiar voice and Sarah looked up to find Jamie watching her, the oddest expression in his blue eyes.

She looked down again, busy clamping both ends of the umbilical cord, but her hands were

trembling as she turned to the father. 'Would you
like to cut the cord?'

He nodded, wiping the corners of his eyes.
'I'm sorry,' he mumbled apologetically after the
cord had been cut and Sarah was cleaning and
swaddling the baby in a green cloth.

'For what?' asked Jamie. 'Doesn't every man
cry when his child is born?'

In the middle of her post-birth ministrations
Sarah stiffened, his words chilling her as she
recognised their essential truth. For Jamie had
stood here, like this, when his wife had given birth
to *their* Harriet. He had wiped away tears and
cradled the newborn scrap as Johnny Herley was
doing now. And that profound experience that he
had shared with another woman would never go
away, Sarah accepted heavily.

No wonder that their relationship had slipped
into an intimate, more serious, gear almost
immediately. For Jamie was not like the boys she
had dated in the past, who would take you out for
dinner a couple of times and then attempt to
pounce. Jamie was a man, with a man's experience
of life. And of death.

And Jamie had been *married* to Kathy when she
had borne his child, for heaven's sake! He had
probably dated her and courted her slowly, showing both respect and restraint.

Neither of which he had accorded to her.

And in nine months' time, *she* could be lying
there, giving birth to a child conceived when the
father was almost a stranger to her. If she had been

alone at that moment Sarah might have wept at how easily things seemed to have got out of hand.

And Jamie read every thought that was written in Sarah's gorgeous green eyes as clearly as if she had spoken them aloud. Her uncertainty of how much substance their relationship carried and the immense burden of knowing that she could be carrying his child. But he could offer her no words of comfort, not least because it would have been inappropriate in the circumstances, with the new baby bawling its head off in the background. But also because the truth was unpalatable. What could he say to her that would not cause her even more distress? 'I hope for everyone's sake, but especially for Harriet's, that you *aren't* pregnant but if you are I'll stand by you.'

Big deal! 'Do you need me to stay, Sarah?' he asked quite gently.

It sounded to her ears like a loaded question. 'Not just at the moment,' she answered softly, but to her surprise and delight he blew her a kiss as he breezed out of the delivery room.

CHAPTER EIGHT

EARLY on Saturday morning there was a rap-tap-a-tap on Sarah's door and she pulled it open to find Jamie standing there, wearing very pale, beautifully cut trousers and a silk shirt. He looked an absolute knockout and the cornflower-blue of the shirt matched his eyes *exactly*, thought Sarah with hungry amusement.

'Hello,' she said, feeling oddly shy and wondering whether he would kiss her.

'Hi.' His eyes were soft but he made no attempt to take her into his arms.

Swallowing down her disappointment, she peered over his shoulder and frowned. 'Where's Harriet?'

His voice was guarded. He had already had regrets and the day had hardly begun. Just getting Harriet to agree to come had been the biggest tussle of his life. 'She's waiting in the car. She—didn't want to leave Blue. I'm sorry.'

Which, translated, probably meant that she did not want to see Sarah's home, she supposed. 'Oh, well,' said Sarah brightly. 'That doesn't matter! It's such a beautiful day we ought to get going anyway!' She felt a bit of a fool. She had spent ages making the small flat look like home and there were three empty milk bottles containing

141

bunches of flowers that she had bought in Southbury yesterday. She really *must* get herself a vase!

She had also bought several different types of fruit juice and some chocolate croissants, just in case Harriet was hungry. And a book featuring all the stained-glass windows of Southbury Cathedral, with some felt-tips for her to colour it in. Oh, well. They would keep. Or maybe she was too old for colouring? Her own niece, Sammi, who was only a year younger than Harriet, simply *loved* colouring. But then all children were, she supposed, quite different.

'Shall we go?' asked Jamie politely, wondering why on earth he had suggested this type of day out so early on. He had seen a new emotion in Harriet's eyes that morning—an understandable but unattractive emotion—jealousy. He just hoped that she would not make it as obvious to Sarah as she had to him.

'Yes, let's go,' answered Sarah equally politely, and shut the door behind her.

He glanced at her as they walked down to the car. The weather forecast was good and she was wearing the most simple sleeveless dress in a kind of apple-green linen. It was short—well above the knee—and showed off her gorgeous, athletic legs which were lightly tanned. On her feet were strappy, brown leather sandals which tied halfway up her calf and looked like the kind of footwear seen in illustrations of the Greek gods! Her finger, he noted, was covered in a protective plaster.

'What have you done to your finger?'

'Oh, that.' She regarded the injured digit ruefully. 'I cut it on a photo frame.' In her great blitz on the flat she had knocked her favourite photograph flying and smashed the glass. It featured her niece Sammi, tightly holding her new baby brother, Sebastian, Sarah's godson. Her brother Ben and his wife, Verity, had given it to Sarah as a farewell present just before she started at Southbury. The silver frame was, thankfully, unmarked and so was the photo but as Sarah was carefully picking out shards of glass from the carpet she had lanced her finger.

'Deep cut, is it?'

'No.'

'And are you up to date on tetanus?'

Sarah met his eyes. 'Yes, Doctor,' she answered solemnly and he saw her lips twitch and they both started laughing.

They were still laughing when they reached the car and the first thing that Sarah saw was the angry and indignant look on Harriet's face, as though her father had no right to be laughing with another woman. She's hurt and jealous, thought Sarah. And she's only nine with no mother. I must remember that.

'Hello, Harriet!' she smiled but Harriet just stared at her blankly as though she had not heard her speak.

'Say hello to Sarah, Harriet,' said Jamie, glowering at the sullen face of his daughter.

'"Hello to Sarah!"' mimicked the nine-year-old in an infuriating sing-song voice.

Jamie threw Sarah an apologetic glance and opened his mouth to speak but almost imperceptibly she shook her head. Let's just leave it, her eyes told him.

He gave a small nod, then leaned down to speak to his daughter. 'Are you going to get in the back with Blue?' he queried softly. 'And let Sarah sit in the front?'

Brown eyes were fixed levelly on Sarah. 'Why? Don't you like dogs?'

Sarah nodded. 'I love dogs——'

'Harriet,' Jamie interrupted with an impatient growl, 'just move, will you?'

'No,' said Sarah firmly, determined not to create waves where they could be avoided. 'I'll be fine in the back. Honestly.'

Famous last words! If only she had realised that the Jag, though an amazingly powerful car which was heaven to be driven in, *was* primarily a two-seater she would never have offered! A slender nine-year-old like Harriet would have had difficulty hunching up in the back but for a well-built girl like Sarah it was sheer hell! Especially with a stale-breathed dog trying to lick at her face every two seconds!

'Are you OK back there, Sarah?' asked Harriet innocently.

'Absolutely fine,' answered Sarah from between gritted teeth as she gave Blue's wet nose a gentle shove.

'Oh, please don't push Blue,' reprimanded

Harriet querulously. 'She can't *help* it if her breath smells; she *has* just been terribly ill, hasn't she, Daddy?'

'Mmm,' answered Jamie noncommitally, meeting Sarah's eyes in his rear-view mirror with a mixture of resignation and amusement.

'Where are we going?' asked Sarah, slightly mollified by that look in his eyes.

'I'd planned a walk in Foreman Forest,' said Jamie. 'It's a local beauty spot—only about twenty miles outside Southbury and quite exquisite.'

'Sounds great,' said Sarah.

'There's a restaurant on the outskirts of the forest, which I *had* thought we could try for lunch, but—'

'I didn't want to leave Blue in the car,' piped up Harriet immediately. 'It isn't fair—especially when she's just been ill.'

'So Harriet has packed us all a picnic,' announced Jamie, with a comically warning look at Sarah in the mirror. 'And I allowed her the responsibility of choosing everything herself!'

'Should be fun! What did you pack, Harriet?' asked Sarah, trying very hard to be positive. 'I *adore* picnics!'

'You'll have to wait and see!' announced Harriet gleefully.

The day was not a success.

In fact, thought Sarah as she gamely forced herself to eat a second peanut-butter-and-pickle sandwich, it was an out-and-out disaster!

First of all Blue disappeared into the forest and

it took an age to find her and when they did she refused to walk back with them, which meant that Jamie had to carry her. Blue was not a big dog but she was certainly a very heavy one.

'You'll have to put this dog on a diet, Harry!' he complained.

'She eats for comfort because you're hardly ever home,' said Harriet innocently, turning her most winning smile on her father. 'She gets just as lonely as *I* do!'

And by the time they had got Blue back into the car and driven to a pretty clearing for lunch it had begun to bucket down with rain.

Sarah was sure that there must be worse places to eat a picnic lunch than cramped in the back of a steaming Jag with the rain lashing around outside but right now she was darned if she could think of one!

Jamie was trying his best to conceal his irritation but failing miserably, while Harriet was openly triumphant at the way events were going.

Much more of this, thought Sarah, and the two of them would come to blows! It's up to *me*, decided Sarah determinedly, to pep things up a bit.

'So, what's for pudding?' she queried brightly.

'Chocolate yoghurt,' answered Harriet guilelessly. 'But I'm afraid it hasn't been in the fridge so it's a bit warm. Here——' and she thrust the lukewarm plastic container into Sarah's hand.

Sarah felt that she deserved a medal for managing to plough her way through the warmest, runniest, sickliest yoghurt she could ever have imagined eating and it didn't help when Harriet's arm jogged her and half the carton plopped onto Sarah's apple-green linen dress.

It was the final straw and as she dabbed at it impotently with a paper napkin she wished that she could just get out of the car and walk back to the nurses' home. What was the use? she thought. Her eyes were perilously close to filling with tears and she deliberately refused to look at either Jamie or Harriet for fear that she would start blubbing.

'Is your dress ruined?' enquired Harriet.

'Very probably,' answered Sarah equably, no mean feat considering that she felt like screaming at the top of her voice. And she wasn't going to say that it didn't matter because it did! That linen dress had cost her a fortune!

'Never mind!' said Harriet brightly. 'You can change it when we drop you off. We are going to drop Sarah off now, aren't we, Daddy?'

'No,' answered Jamie flatly. He could never remember having felt such a blind, cold rage towards his daughter for her deliberate attempts to ruin their day. And no matter how much he tried to rationalise it the anger just would *not* go away which, in turn, made him feel guilty. He sighed, wondering anew whether it was worth all this aggravation. Perhaps this was fate taking a hand, telling him that he would be more fulfilled putting his heart and soul into his work instead of upsetting his family dynamics by trying to forge a relationship with another woman which seemed to have the odds stacked up against it from the outset.

And then he caught a glimpse of Sarah's bent head as she pretended to stroke the dog. He could tell from the stiff set of her shoulders how upset she was and a warm rush of protectiveness flooded his veins. 'No,' he said again. 'We're not taking Sarah home.'

'We're not?' asked Sarah and Harriet in unison.

'No. You're going to the cinema with Marianne for the afternoon.'

'You never told me *that*!' complained Harriet sulkily.

'Well, I'm telling you *now*!' retorted Jamie, and Harriet seemed to appreciate that she had pushed her father too far for she lapsed into a discontented silence.

In fact, Jamie had only made the arrangement with Marianne as a back-up plan, just in case Harriet proved difficult. How very prophetic of him!

Consequently, Marianne shot him an understanding glance when the Jag pulled into her father's drive and, after she had sent Harriet off into the kitchen with a promise that they would make toffee together, she gave Sarah a wide, ultra-friendly smile and told them cheerfully to go off and enjoy themselves.

But the tense silence in the car did not bode well for much enjoyment, thought Sarah gloomily as Jamie accelerated away down the drive. He did not say a single word as he skilfully negotiated a tight corner, the red car pulling away with a powerful, throbbing purr.

'Where are we going?' asked Sarah, when she could bear the silence no longer.

He was still so seething with anger and guilt that his answer was a short, terse, 'Home,' and the brooding quality of his reply made Sarah admit to herself just what a disaster the day had been and she gloomily sat back in her seat and pretended to watch the passing traffic.

Let Jamie take the lead, she thought with a faint flare of rebellion as she stared dismally at her dress—at the pale brown circle which was the legacy of the spilt yoghurt. Was the relationship, like the dress, probably spoiled for ever?

After about ten minutes of non-communication Jamie drove down a leafy, tree-lined road which, for all its abundant greenery, was only a relatively short distance from the city centre. He drew up in front of a large Edwardian house set within its own walled garden and Blue began to wag her tail in anticipation.

'We're here,' he announced somewhat unnecessarily, but he was feeling a mixture of delicious anticipation and nervous excitment. What would her reaction be to him bringing her here? he wondered.

'Here?' Sarah murmured, for she had half expected to be dropped off at the nurses' home. 'Where's here?'

'Where I live.' He climbed out of the car and Blue jumped out after him. Then he came round to open Sarah's door for her and offered her his hand to help her out. But when she gave it to him he did not release it but raised it slowly to his lips and kissed the palm, quite, quite tenderly, and all Sarah's doubts just vanished as he pulled her into his arms and brought his mouth down on hers.

He was woken by the sound of a blackbird singing directly outside his bedroom window and Jamie opened his eyes to see that the clock read four o'clock. When was the last time he had made love in the afternoon? he asked himself with sleepy satisfaction. He gave a lazy smile as he stretched, glancing at the sleeping form of Sarah beside him as he did so.

Beneath the sheet she was was completely naked and Jamie felt the excitement stir him as his gaze rested on the tantalising curve of her breasts that jutted proudly against the fine white linen.

One arm was bent carelessly above her head and the rich, dark silk of her hair spilled in glorious disarray over the pillow. Her skin was so soft to the touch and so sweet to the taste, he remembered with a pang which made him long for her even more.

He was just about to start making love to her all over again when the shrill of the bleeper broke into his sensual thoughts like a masked intruder. *Now* what was going on? he wondered, irritated by the unwelcome interruption.

With a reluctantly stifled groan he lifted the receiver and punched out the number to the hospital.

'Mr Brennan,' he said abruptly. 'Who's bleeping me?'

'It's the O and G registrar,' answered the operator. 'Dr Alcott.'

'But I'm not on call,' pointed out Jamie, 'and neither is Dr Alcott.'

'He just asked to speak to you,' said the operator smoothly in a don't-ask-me-I'm-just-doing-my-job voice.

'OK,' Jamie sighed, sensing that objection would get him nowhere. 'Put him through.'

'Just a moment, Mr Brennan.'

While he waited for the connection Jamie remembered that he had intended going for a drink with Aidan Alcott, who had obviously been under stress. And he hadn't. There had been no time. No time to do anything properly, he thought.

Dr Aidan Alcott came on the phone, his voice sounding stressed and almost tearful. 'C-can I see you please, Jamie? It's important.'

Jamie frowned as he snatched a longing glance at Sarah. He felt only compassion for his colleague but to say that now was not the greatest time in the world was putting it mildly! 'When?'

'N-now. I wouldn't ask only it's—important.'

Jamie looked again at Sarah who was now stirring slightly in sleep, a beatific smile curving her luscious lips, and then her green eyes snapped open and she looked startled to find him leaning on his elbow, watching her. He leaned forward to gently kiss the end of her nose, then spoke into the receiver. 'I'll be there in half an hour,' he said reluctantly. 'Meet me in the doctors' office on Starling ward.'

Sarah's bubble of happiness burst immediately. Why, in heaven's name, was he planning to go off to the hospital? *Now*?

Jamie put the phone down and leaned over her. 'Hello,' he said softly.

'Hello,' she answered, but her reply was guarded.

Jamie knew exactly why. 'Darling, the last thing in the world I want to do is to go in.'

'Is it an emergency?'

He shook his head. 'No. Well, not really.'

'Then why?'

He shrugged. 'I think my registrar is going through some kind of crisis in his life. He didn't say exactly what the matter was but he sounded pretty het-up. Sarah, I have to go.'

'I suppose so.' She was horrified to hear how petulant and protesting she sounded but she couldn't seem to stop herself. Because, for once in her life, she felt hard-done-by. Selfish it might be but she found herself wondering why *she* couldn't come first for once, instead of work and his daughter and now, it seemed, his registrar too?

He tilted her chin with one long forefinger so that their eyes met, his blue and dazzling with a hint of regretful laughter lurking in their depths.

'Darling, no one could be more disappointed than I am. I had planned to make love to you again and then I was going to open a bottle of champagne and feed you various delicacies from the fridge with my fingers. You were—are—an amazing woman, Sarah. Do you know that?' His voice deepened to a sultry whisper.

Sarah's green eyes softened and her cheeks went very pink and she couldn't think of a single thing to say!

'You are also the first woman who has ever been here with me like this.' It seemed important that he told her that.

'Don't tell me—you only moved in last week?' joked Sarah, seeking refuge in humour because otherwise she was terribly afraid that she was going to dissolve into a terrible emotional mess.

'A year ago,' he told her unwaveringly.

She dared to ask the question which she knew she had no right to ask. 'And has there been— anyone else—since Kathy died?'

This was a tricky one to answer. But he was clear about one thing. He shook his head. 'Not in the way you mean, no.'

Something in the evasive way he answered had her digging for more. 'But there was someone that you were—fond of?' She couldn't bring herself to say *in love with* because Sarah had realised in his arms that afternoon that she wanted him to love *her*. And her alone.

Jamie nodded, remembering how Verity had helped him through the really bad times after Kathy had died. How she and her daughter had taken Harriet under their wing; had entertained her and welcomed her into their home while her mother lay at home dying. And when the pain had

gone away Jamie had seen Verity for what she
was—a beautiful, warm and sensitive woman
whom Harriet adored. How easy it would have
been if she had not been in love with someone
else. . .

'Yes,' he answered slowly. 'Someone I was very
fond of.'

But it was Sarah who was here now. Sarah who
was beside him. Sarah who was in his arms. Sarah
who he had just made love to. Very quickly Sarah
seemed to have become the focus of his entire
world. He kissed her very thoroughly and then
groaned as he moved away from her, knowing that
he had to stop or. . .

He climbed out of bed, completely at home with
his nakedness, a rueful expression on his face as
he followed the shocked and startled direction of
her eyes. 'Yes, you've turned me on, Sarah,' he
teased softly. '*Really* turned me on. Satisfied?'

'Not really,' she murmured, her dark lashes flut-
tering to conceal the hectic emerald gleam in
her eyes.

He laughed, his voice breaking slightly on a
husky note of desire, before glancing at his watch
as if it were a poisoned chalice. 'Darling, I must
take a shower.'

Sarah must have drifted off to sleep for she was
still in bed when he returned, unsure of what they
were going to do next though that soon became
very clear.

'I guess I'd better drop you off on the way in
to the hospital,' he said, slightly apologetically.

'I've no idea how long I'll be.'

'Oh. Right.' Sarah felt awkward as she climbed out of bed.

'Have a shower.'

'No.' She shook her head and pulled on her underwear. 'I'll have one when I get home.'

He had begun to make the bed, a resigned expression in his eyes, when he caught her watching him and he paused in the act of straightening the rumpled duvet. 'In case Harriet gets home before I do,' he explained uncomfortably and then, feeling that perhaps she deserved to be confronted with the truth, however unpalatable, he put on a false American accent as if doing that would somehow lessen the blow. 'You know that if you stick with me, kid, then there won't be many afternoons where we can just go to bed like this?' he drawled.

Sarah nodded, though she didn't quite understand. He seemed to be promising her something and yet warning her at the same time that it might not be what she wanted. Or maybe what *he* wanted? Was *that* it?

Jamie saw the regretful look on her face and wondered whether he should even be *trying* to court a woman like Sarah. Was it asking too much of her? She would never have those wild, carefree days with him—long weekends spent in bed together with the rest of the world locked out. Should he be sensible and look towards a woman who had children of her own—who knew the joy and the heartbreak and the inevitable restrictions on freedom? Someone like Verity?

He thought back to the woman he had wanted to spend his life with before she had gone off and married the only man she had ever really loved.

And, not for the first time, he wondered how he would feel if he came face to face with Verity now.

CHAPTER NINE

SARAH arrived back at her flat at five o'clock with the prospect of a long, long evening ahead of her. Jamie had given her a long, hard goodbye kiss as he had dropped her off but there had been no mention of when they might meet up again.

'I'll ring you,' he had said, and that had been that.

She looked out of the window, at where the cathedral's pointed tip was etched against the golden-blue of the summer sky, wondering what to do with the rest of her evening. She supposed that she could venture down into Southbury to explore. Or go to the nurses' television room and try to make a few friends.

She suddenly felt quite lonely and a wave of homesickness propelled her into the corridor where she found the pay-phone, now mercifully working, and called her parents.

'Mum?' she said tentatively when she heard the connection being made.

'Sarah?' Her mother's voice was perceptively shrill. 'Is everything all right?'

Sarah fought down the urge to confide. Her mother would only worry and, besides, she was a grown woman—she couldn't go running to her mother every time she had problems. Not these kind of problems, anyway. 'Everything's just fine, Mum!' she answered.

'Good.' Mrs Jackson clearly had other things on her mind. 'I've got some news for you, darling— Maisy has just got engaged!'

Sarah's heart sank at the news. Maisy was Sarah's brilliant surgeon sister and was the most gorgeous creature on earth. Unfortunately, she also happened to have the most dreary boyfriend ever invented. 'Not *Giles*?' she asked, with a groan.

'Of *course* it's Giles!' answered her mother indignantly. 'I don't know what you others seem to have against him—he's a very nice man!'

'Exactly!' said Sarah gloomily. Whoever wanted to marry a 'very nice man'?

'Anyway,' said her mother, changing the subject, 'we're having a surprise party for them both next Saturday. Can you come?'

Sarah thought about it. 'Actually, I can. I'm off for the whole weekend.'

'Come and stay then,' said Mrs Jackson immediately, sounding pleased. 'We miss having you around the place, darling.'

Sarah hesitated. 'Um, Mum, would it be, I mean, could I bring someone?'

'Of course you can bring someone! Who is it, a man?'

'Mmm.' Sarah felt slightly distracted, wondering how best to tell her mother. Straight out, no doubt. 'Um—the only thing is—'

'Yes, dear?'

'—that he's got a daughter—'

'A daughter?' interjected Mrs Jackson sharply. 'Why? Is he divorced?'

'No,' answered Sarah heavily, wishing to high heaven that she had never brought the subject up. 'He's a widower, actually.'

'And how old is he?'

'About thirty-four—'

'*About*? You mean you don't know?'

'I mean we haven't really gotten around to discussing it—'

'Oh!' interrupted her mother cheerfully, and Sarah could almost *hear* her mother thinking, It can't be *that* serious, then! 'Then, by all means, bring him as well, dear—and his daughter, too, if she wants to come. Plenty of room here—you know that. How old is she?'

'She's nine,' answered Sarah.

'Hmm. He married quite young, then,' observed her mother. 'You know, Sarah, it might be nice if you *did* bring her—it would be someone for Sammi to play with.'

'Well, we'll see,' said Sarah noncommittally. She couldn't imagine her bubbly niece getting on with Harriet at all. 'Oh, and, Mum. Just one thing. You won't tell the others, will you?' Sarah adored her three sisters and brother and their various spouses but they really were the most shocking gossips. And what if Jamie refused point blank to go? What a fool she would look then. 'He might not want to come.'

'I won't breathe a word to anyone, dear. I shall

be much too busy preparing a feast for Maisy and Giles!'

'Bye, Mum,' said Sarah and she put the phone down, wondering, not for the first time, just how her sister could marry someone with a name like *Giles*!

The next few days were a frustrating mixture of elation and despair for Sarah.

Work was fantastic, reminding Sarah of why she had gone into midwifery in the first place. The maternity unit at Southbury was brilliantly run by Sister Singleton and in her first week there Sarah found it busy, stimulating and varied, with Sister still allowing her to 'float'—to work on the wards that needed her most.

If only her social life was similarly fantastic, she thought wistfully. She had not seen Jamie alone to talk to since the day of the picnic. He had shot her a few helpless looks from across the ward, usually when he was dashing up to Theatre or gowning up to deliver a breech baby or multiple birth. Every time they got within chatting distance another member of staff would appear or Sarah would be rung by a patient or Jamie's bleeper would shrill demandingly. Sometimes Sarah found herself wondering whether there was a conspiracy against them ever being alone together!

Yesterday she had seen him speeding up to Theatre as she had been coming off duty. 'I'll ring you later!' he had called, but he had not rung her and Sarah's filthy temper was only slightly improved by one of the other nurses on her corridor telling her that the pay-phone had been broken into yet again. So maybe he *had* tried to get through to her.

And it didn't seem to matter how much she told herself that it wasn't as though he did not have commitments. That he couldn't just come and see her in the evening unless he had arranged a baby-sitter—which wasn't always easy. She didn't just feel like second best at the moment—she felt like third or fourth best!

Consequently she had to make a real effort to lift her mood when she walked onto the antenatal ward the following morning.

The work on the antenatal ward, where pregnant women were admitted, tended to be fairly routine with the midwives observing the mothers-to-be for a variety of reasons. One woman was expecting triplets; another had a poor obstetric history; yet another had a Shirodkar suture that needed removing. One thing that they all had in common was the possibility that they might have a difficult labour and birth. Being in the controlled surroundings of a hospital *before* they went into labour meant that the staff could anticipate problems before they arose and act on them.

It was known affectionately as the ward of moans—since most of the women were heavily pregnant and just looking forward to having their babies and going home!

After she had been given report Sarah went round the ward doing her observations, finally getting to Mrs Simpson—a lady whom Jamie had admitted the day before from his clinic with what was called a transverse lie. This meant that the baby was lying in the womb on its side instead of the usual position of head first. Sarah knew that it was best to admit the patient so that she could be properly assessed and observed and a cause for the malpresentation of the baby could be investigated.

'Hi, Mrs Simpson!' greeted Sarah, and Mrs Simpson put down the magazine she had been trying unsuccessfully to read.

'Oh, hello, Staff!' she said, rather tiredly.

Sarah took out the old-fashioned trumpet which was still used for monitoring the baby's heartbeat. 'How are you feeling today?'

Mrs Simpson smiled valiantly. 'Uncomfortable. Hot. Tired. Fed up to the back teeth with being in hospital!'

'Let's hope it's not too much longer, then!' And, as Sarah spoke, Mrs Simpson's membranes ruptured all over the bed. There was water everywhere and Mrs Simpson blinked at Sarah in confusion. 'What's happened?'

'Your waters have gone!' Sarah supplied briefly as she hurried into action, trying to be both speedily efficient and yet calm at the same time so as not to alarm her patient. 'I'm going to have to examine you, Mrs Simpson,' she told her. She needed to check that the umbilical cord had not slipped down or prolapsed. Prolapse was much more common in malpresentation of the foetus and the cord slipping down could cause a lack of vital oxygen supply to the baby, particularly if part of the baby was actually compressing the cord.

Sarah lifted up the sheet, took one look at Mrs Simpson and bit back a yelp. She had read about prolapsed cords but this was the first time she had actually witnessed one for herself.

She could see the umbilical cord, with its three vessels making it look like a twisted rope and its jelly-like covering which resembled aspic.

But what was more important and more pressing, literally, was that Sarah could also see the baby's head, and she needed to stop it from compressing the cord itself.

With her index finger she pushed the baby's head back and yelled loudly for Sister. 'Please keep as still as you are, Mrs Simpson,' she urged. 'Baby's on its way and we may have to take you up to Theatre!'

Sister appeared at that moment, with Jamie behind her, and neither of them needed to ask Sarah what the matter was. They both looked to see Sarah frantically pushing the baby's head away with her finger and could have made a diagnosis from that, even if they hadn't seen the cord.

'Right. Ring Theatre and tell them to prepare for a case, would you, Hilary?' barked out Jamie, and leant over Mrs Simpson as Sister scurried out of the cubicle again. 'Your cord is pushing down,' he explained. 'Do you remember I told you in clinic that a cord prolapse was a possible cause of your baby lying that way?'

'Yes,' gasped Mrs Simpson.

'That's what's happening. You need to go to Theatre and have a Caesarean. Right now.'

'Are you going to do it, Mr Brennan?' the patient gasped tremulously.

'Too right I am!' and Mrs Simpson actually managed a smile.

The porter arrived and he, Jamie and Sarah trundled the trolley up to Theatre. Speed was of the essence and Sarah knew that she would never forget that journey for as long as she lived, with her still pushing frantically against the baby's head with all her might. It was physically quite a tough task and once or twice Jamie glanced at her.

'Want me to take over?'

She shook her head. 'I'm fine. Save your strength for operating.'

He shot her a brief, grateful smile as the lift doors closed behind them.

The theatre staff were expecting them and they were rushed straight through into the anaesthetic room. 'The things you have to do to get attention!' joked Mrs Simpson weakly.

Sarah stayed in position from when they anaesthetised Mrs Simpson and prepared the operation site to when Jamie made a sure and clean abdominal incision.

And all the theatre staff who were assisting gave an involuntary round of applause as a wriggling baby girl was lifted free to open her lungs and squawk most indignantly!

Sarah had cleaned up and was waiting to accompany Mrs Simpson and her new daughter

(provisionally called Sarah!) back to the ward
when she saw Jamie walking quickly down the
corridor, still with his theatre gown beneath his
white coat.

He looked tired, she thought. Dog tired.

He gave something resembling a smile as he
approached. 'Can't stop—I'm needed on the
gynae ward urgently. A girl of sixteen is bleeding
very badly and we don't know why. I'll see you
later, Sarah. Oh, and thanks. Once again—you
were superb!'

But it wasn't until Sarah was coming off duty
that she bumped into Jamie. It had been a fairly
traumatic afternoon and she had had her own
problems on the ward, with a young woman haem-
orrhaging heavily after delivering a healthy baby.

And now, alone in the corridor with him, she
suddenly felt peculiarly shy but, much more than
that, outrageously pleased to see him.

Jamie looked her up and down, noting the dark
shadows that bruised the delicate skin beneath her
bright green eyes. 'You look bushed,' he said.

'So do you,' she answered softly.

'Yeah.' He paused, wondering how much of his
ongoing problems to burden her with! But he really
did owe her some kind of explanation. 'I'm sorry
I haven't been in touch,' he began.

Sarah shook her dark head. 'It doesn't matter—'

'Yes,' he interrupted gently, 'it does. Your
phone was broken—'

'I know, Jamie,' she said softly.

'My registrar has taken sick leave,' he told her.

'I recommended that he should.'

'Oh?'

'He's been under a lot of stress. His mother died last year and his wife is a also a doctor—only she's doing her house jobs miles away. So Aidan spends all his spare time travelling to see her and then, when he gets there he's so exhausted that he either falls asleep or they spend their whole time arguing! He needs to rest and to get his life sorted out before he can deal with other people's problems.'

He ran his hand abstractedly through his thick, dark hair. 'I also had to go and see Harriet's school-teacher last night.' He met the question in her eyes with a shrug. 'Her work has been falling off and they wanted to know why.' He didn't mention that he had had to deal with a stony-faced, mealy-mouthed old biddy who had spent the entire interview firing instrusively personal questions at him.

He remembered the prim way that she had said, 'We often find, Mr Brennan, that children of single-parent families tend to over-react if *another woman* is introduced into their lives too soon.' And the patronising question in her eyes.

Jamie had felt like storming out. Or like standing there and asking her who the hell she thought she was; that it wasn't 'too soon'; that it had been four years since Kathy had died and he was only thirty-three, for God's sake, and his life wasn't over!

Kathy, herself, he thought with sad affection, wouldn't want it to be.

He made up his mind that he would go and see the headmistress to complain about the teacher's attitude. When he got the time.

He looked into slanting green eyes and made his mind up.

This weekend, he thought. He would see if Harriet could stay over with Marianne. Then he could wine and dine Sarah. Take her to bed; talk to her, even. Oh, yes. Suddenly he just wanted to talk and talk to her and never stop. There was something soft and sweet and vulnerable at the very core of her; something that invited confidences he had never before wanted to give, even to Verity. And he wanted to question her—to probe and to find out what made her tick. He wanted to hear all about her sunny childhood and her family.

Sarah looked at the harsh lines of worry which gave his face such a tense look and suddenly she just wanted to hold him in her arms; to cradle him and comfort him until all the tension was simply washed away.

'Sarah—'

'Jamie—'

They both spoke at the same time and then laughed, slightly self-consciously.

'You first,' he said.

She drew a deep breath. 'My sister has just got engaged—the guy's a bit of a creep but you can't have everything! Anyway, the thing is that my parents are arranging a surprise party for them this weekend coming and I sort of wondered if you'd like to—' she gave a tentative smile '—come with me?'

Jamie's heart sank but he just managed to keep the smile on his face. He had rather wanted to be alone with her but the party obviously meant a lot to her and the fact that she wanted to introduce him to her family was a good sign. And their cosy weekend would keep. . .

'Love to,' he said.

'I phoned my mother and told her I might be bringing someone. She said. . .' Sarah hesitated, not wanting it to sound as though she was being pushy '. . .she said that you're very welcome to bring Harriet if she wants to come.'

Jamie thought about it. Harriet had been giving him cause for concern for a while now but his relationship with Sarah had only exacerbated it. Sooner rather than later he was going to have to deal with it. But not now. And not this weekend, either. He could not cope with Harriet creating a scene at Sarah's parents'.

'It's very sweet of you and of your mother to offer,' he told her. 'And please thank her. But perhaps it might be an idea if she went to stay with Marianne and her family. That way—' and his eyes crinkled with sensual suggestion '—we might be able to snatch a little time alone together.' He saw her face, trying her best not to look crestfallen, and he could have kicked himself.

'I don't just mean making love to you, Sarah,'

he added gently. 'Although I have to admit that
making love features pretty high on the "things I
would like to do with Sarah Jackson" list that I
compiled first thing this morning when I was lying
awake thinking about you. But what I would also
like to do is to talk to you or not talk to you as
the mood takes us. To lounge around on the sofa
drinking wine and listening to music. Without
being interrupted by bleepers or phones or daughters. Normal things which most people take for
granted. Now how does that sound to you?'

It sounded like bliss.

And just the thought of it made Sarah almost
dizzy with excitement.

CHAPTER TEN

SARAH and Jamie almost didn't get to the party. Jamie's opposite number and his team were stuck in Theatre doing an extremely complicated and time-consuming gynaecological operation when a pregnant woman was brought into Casualty following a car crash. As the on-call team were occupied it was naturally Jamie who was called.

The woman was only thirty-two weeks pregnant but the trauma of the crash and the blood loss that she had suffered were enough to bring on premature labour so Jamie was called for. The woman was far too weak to deliver the baby herself so he ended up having to do an emergency Caesarean.

So that when they should have been driving up the motorway Jamie was still in his theatre gown.

And when they should have been in Sarah's parents' spacious sitting room, raising their glasses and shrieking, '*Surprise*!' to the happy couple at the tops of their voices Jamie was suturing up the incision he had made and trying to keep the tears from his eyes.

Because the baby had died minutes after birth.

At least the mother had survived, he thought grimly. Though, later on, someone was going to have to break the news to her. And it really ought to be him.

He waited until she was back on the ward and relatively comfortable after some post-operative analgesia before he broke the sad news to her and then sat, just silently holding her hand, until her sobbing had subsided.

He waited until the woman's husband had arrived before he took his leave and when he glanced up at the ward clock and saw what the time was he swore softly under his breath. One of the nurses raised her eyes in curious query to the ward sister. Fancy Mr Brennan *swearing*! the expression seemed to say.

He tore his white coat off just as the phone on the wall rang and the nurse answered.

'For you, Mr Brennan,' she said.

It was Sarah. A Sarah who sounded as though she was only holding onto her temper with difficulty. 'Jamie, the party will be almost over by the time we get there——'

'I'm on my way,' he said immediately.

As had happened before there was no time to go home and change and so Jamie opted for what was in his 'emergency' supply in the theatre changing-room. Unfortunately it was a shirt of dazzling turquoise raw silk, worn with close-fitting white jeans. Trendy, yes. Flattering, certainly. But not really what he would have chosen to wear for a formal black-tie dinner! Still, it couldn't be helped. He hoped that Sarah's family could understand that a little rule-breaking was necessary once in a while!

Sarah was waiting downstairs for him by the lift. She wore her shiny hair piled high and was wearing a narrow Chinese dress in jade-green brocade which came to just above her knees. At her ears dangled the jade earrings which jangled as she shook her head a little on catching sight of Jamie.

'You look gorgeous,' he breathed appreciatively.

Sarah burst out laughing. 'And *you*,' she giggled, 'look as if you're just off on your summer holidays!'

'Will your folks mind?'

'They will,' she said, firmly taking him by the arm and propelling him towards the glass doors, 'if we're very much later! So, move it, Jamie Brennan!'

Jamie was terribly aware of having left all his responsibilities behind for once and he felt positively light-hearted. Harriet and Blue were in marvellous hands at Marianne's. His bleeper was turned off. Nothing and no one could touch him until he arrived back tomorrow evening. Except for Sarah, of course. She could touch him as much as she liked. He shot her a sideways glance, loving the pure, clean lines of her straight nose and pert little jaw and the way that the upswept hairstyle emphasised the swan-like curve of her long neck.

'Do you realise that we're going to be able to have an uninterrupted conversation for once?' he asked, when they were finally on the motorway.

'That, in itself, should be enough to make us both clam up!' Sarah giggled.

'True,' he laughed, thinking how little he knew about her—other than what a wicked sense of humour she had. 'So, tell me about your family.'

'Where shall I start? It's a pretty big family—three sisters and a brother.'

'What about your folks?'

'Mum used to be a nurse and Dad's a doctor—or rather he was; he's retired now.'

Jamie frowned. It was the first he had heard that her father was a doctor. But then he had never asked her before—and why would she bother mentioning it? 'Not James Jackson?' he queried in surprise. 'The surgeon?'

'The very same,' smiled Sarah proudly. 'It's nice that you've heard of him.'

'Who hasn't?' asked Jamie. 'The work he did on small intestine surgery was mould-breaking!' Another, faintly warning, bell rang deep in the recesses of his mind but Sarah chose just that moment to cross one elegant black-stockinged leg over its partner and Jamie's mind lost all thoughts other than how much he would like to pull over and kiss her.

It was almost ten by the time they drove up the long, gravel drive and pulled up in front of one of the most beautiful houses that Jamie had ever seen.

'Wow,' he said softly. 'What an amazing place!'

'Come *on*!' said Sarah, mock scoldingly.

He held her hand as they walked towards the building, where lights were blazing from every

room, and he wished to high heaven that they were
slipping off somewhere, just the two of them.

Although she had her own key Sarah rang the
doorbell as it seemed rather rude to merely stroll
into an engagement party! After a couple of
minutes her mother appeared at the door, resplen-
dent in buttercup-yellow silk.

'Darling!' she cried.

'Mummy, you look lovely,' smiled Sarah. 'And
this is Jamie Brennan.'

'I'm delighted to meet you, Mrs Jackson,' said
Jamie and shook her by the hand. He smiled. 'You
must forgive me for my somewhat unconventional
attire but I had to step in and operate unexpectedly.
Consequently, I had to come straight from Theatre
and my emergency supply of clothes didn't quite
run to a formal dinner suit!'

Mrs Jackson gave the tall man in front of her a
shrewd and narrow-eyed scrutiny and then, quite
suddenly, she smiled hugely and Sarah got the
distinct feeling that Jamie had just passed some
kind of unspoken test. 'Call me Lizzy,' she urged.
'And come and meet the rest of the family! Maisy
has disappeared—somewhere down the end of the
garden, we think,' she confided. 'Giles has gone
searching for her. They've been rowing all
evening!'

'Promising sign for their forthcoming
marriage!' put in Sarah with caustic humour.

They followed Mrs Jackson into the room where
she was immediately collared by a flustered wait-
ress. As Sarah walked into the large, crowded

drawing-room with Jamie close behind her conversation became more muted and then resumed but all Sarah could register was Jamie's inexplicable reaction to something in the room.

He had stiffened and his eyes were fixed in disbelief on a person standing at the far side of the room. Sarah followed the direction of his eyes to see her sister-in-law, Verity, wearing a spangly silver dress and with a glass of champagne frozen midway to her lips. And nearby Verity's husband, Ben, was watching the proceedings with a watchful, interested gaze.

What the hell was going on?

Suddenly Jamie took Sarah's elbow and swiftly led her back out into the hall. He glanced around, found a closed door, checked inside and, on finding it empty, pushed Sarah into the room.

It was a book-lined study and Jamie didn't even bother switching the light on—the full moon outside the uncurtained window was illumination enough.

It was like walking into some awful dream. The pieces of the puzzle came together. Drawing a deep, ragged breath, he turned on her angrily. 'You're Benedict Jackson's sister,' he accused flatly.

In the mists of confusion a coherent thought began to clamour to be heard and Sarah stared long and hard at Jamie as bits of half-remembered conversation came flitting back to her. When Ben had first met Verity. . .hadn't there been another man she was involved with? A man with a child?

Jamie?

His mouth had hardened into an unrecognisably angry line. 'Why didn't you tell me that you were Verity's sister-in-law?' he demanded harshly, thinking that fate could not have dealt him a worse hand.

Sarah saw the pain and misery on his face and that look produced the death-knell to all her hopes and dreams.

'Is this your idea of a joke?' he demanded, when still she didn't speak. 'To bring me here like this and spring it on me unannounced? *Is it*? Did you know all the time, Sarah?'

Sarah couldn't bear it; she honestly couldn't bear it. She turned on him, her mouth trembling with emotion. 'No! I didn't know!' she stumbled. 'But I'm glad that I didn't! Because at least it enabled to see with my own eyes how stupid I've been! That there's no hope for the two of us—not when you're still so obviously in love with Verity!'

And she ran out of the room and up the vast staircase to her old bedroom where, surrounded by threadbare teddy-bears and rag-dolls, Sarah sobbed hot tears onto her pillow.

The tears had subsided into the occasional sniffle and Sarah was lying on her back staring blankly at the ceiling and wondering what on earth to do next when there was a tap on the door. She sprang to her feet immediately and ran over and yanked the door open, the look of angry anticipation dying on her face when she saw that it was her brother, Ben, who stood there.

His handsome face creased into a sardonic smile as he walked past her and shut the door behind him. 'Sorry, Sarah,' he commented drily. 'It's only me, I'm afraid, not Jamie.'

'I wouldn't want to see him anyway!' she blustered but more treacherous tears spilled down her cheeks. 'Rotten, cheating rat!'

Ben shook his head and handed her a pristine white handkerchief. 'Rubbish,' he remonstrated gently. 'He isn't any of those things and you're clearly in love with the man!'

It was such a relief to be able to admit it. 'How can you tell?' she sniffed.

He gave her a long look. 'Sarah,' he said patiently, 'I've known you all my life, remember?' He sat down on the bed and patted the space next to him. 'Now. The question is, how are we going to resolve this situation?'

'He's probably gone home,' said Sarah disconsolately. 'I stormed out of the study and left him there.'

'He hasn't gone home,' corrected Ben.

She turned tear-stained green eyes on him. 'How do you know?'

'Because he is, at the moment, sitting quietly on the terrace, having a drink and talking to Verity.'

Sarah gazed at him in horror. How could he be so *calm* about it? 'But she's your *wife*!'

Ben smiled. 'Yes, she is. And?'

'And he used to be in love with her!'

'Did he?' He regarded her thoughtfully.

'*Yes*!'

'Are you really quite sure about that? Has he told you?'

'Not in so many words.' Sarah frowned at her brother, wondering how he could be so laid-back about things. '*Ben*! Don't you realise that he could be planning to run off with her at this very moment?' she declared dramatically but, to her astonishment, Ben merely shook his dark head and gave a soft laugh.

'Sarah,' he said, very patiently, 'for Jamie to be able to run off with Verity she would have to want to go with him. And if she wanted to go then her place would not be with me, anyway. Do you see what I'm trying to say?'

'I—think so.'

'I mean that you have to have trust. And I trust Verity.' He took his handkerchief and wiped a dark smudge of mascara from her cheek. 'Has Jamie ever given you the impression of being madly in love with another woman? Be honest now, Sarah.'

She pondered on it. Actually, come to think about it, he had rather given her the impression that he was falling in love with *her*. 'N-no,' she admitted hesitantly.

'There you are, then.'

'But what shall I *do*?' she demanded.

'You ask him for yourself. You let him explain about his relationship with Verity. And you listen to him. Then decide what you want to do. Now—' and he stood up '—go and wash your face, then come downstairs. Act like nothing has happened.

Eat, drink and be merry. Look as though you're having the time of your life. Dance the night away—'

'Oh, but I *can't*, Ben!'

'Oh, but you can,' he corrected acidly. 'Don't crowd Jamie with accusations, Sarah. Let him talk to you in his own good time. He's already been through a lot with Kathy. Seeing Verity unexpectedly must have been an enormous shock for him—as must realising that the woman he had fallen for was the sister of the man he once viewed as his enemy.'

'But not any more?'

'Not any more,' he echoed in agreement. 'Jamie stopped hating me when he realised that I could make Verity happy—he's that kind of person.'

'Do you like him?' asked Sarah suddenly.

Ben smiled. 'I think he's one of the finest men I've ever met,' he answered in a rather gruff and unexpected kind of voice which Sarah had never heard him use before. 'And now I must go down. Your mother has commandeered me to go and search for Maisy.' He gave a dramatic sigh. 'Why is it that the women in this family are so fond of running off?' His mouth curved into a tender smile. 'I'll see you in a minute, little sister.'

Sarah stood up and gazed at him tentatively. 'Do I look all right, Ben?'

Her brother would normally have said something very rude or told her to stop being so vain because, 'Who's going to look at you, anyway?' But now he gave her a long, hard and very critical stare. 'Brush your hair,' he advised curtly, then smiled as he headed for the door. 'And stop *worrying*!'

Jamie put his empty glass down and smiled at Verity as he rose to his feet. 'I must go and find Sarah.'

'Of course you must.' Verity stood up.

'How's the new baby?' he asked.

'Gorgeous. I was very ill when I had him.' Her face held a trace of sadness. 'They tell me I can never have any more children.'

'You have Sammi, too,' he observed quietly.

'Yes.' She paused for a moment, her hair very pale in the moonlight. 'In retrospect it was a mistake to sever all communication between our two girls, you know, Jamie. Harriet was like a big sister to Sammi—it took her a long while to get over it.'

He nodded his head sombrely. 'I know. But think how delighted they're going to be now that they know we've resumed contact!' His blue eyes sparkled with anticipation. 'Maybe being bridesmaids might go some small way towards mollifying them.'

Verity looked at him in surprise. 'Marriage, Jamie?'

'I haven't asked her yet.'

'But you love her?'

'More than I can say.'

'I'm so glad,' she said simply.

He thought how contented she looked, despite

the heartaches of her own life. 'Married life suits you,' he observed.

Verity's face was dreamy. 'Yes. Being married to Benedict is everything I wanted. Only more.'

And suddenly Jamie's need to see Sarah became urgent. 'I'll see you later, Verity,' he said.

He walked back into the drawing-room to see Sarah dancing in the arms of some blond, smooth-looking fellow who stood out by virtue of the fact that he was wearing a tailored white dinner jacket which made him resemble a Hollywood film star.

And suddenly Jamie knew the true meaning of the word jealousy. He found his fist unconsciously clenching and unclenching in the pocket of his trousers and had to take a very deep breath to stop himself from hitting him.

Instead he marched right over to them, put his hand proprietorially around Sarah's waist, gave the blond man a gritted smile and said, 'Excuse me.' Then he shepherded her off the dance-floor with a steely resolve that Sarah found frankly exciting.

He was heading for the front door.

'Where are we going?'

'To talk.' He gave an urbane smile as he saw Ben. 'Please apologise to your parents,' he said pleasantly. 'We'll be back in an hour.'

'I'll say two,' smiled Benedict, with a roguish wink at his sister which made her go a most unflattering brick-red colour.

They got into the car and Jamie started up the engine. 'Where can we go, close by, where we won't be disturbed?' he growled.

Sarah shivered with excitement. 'There's Chenery Peak—it's only a short drive from here.'

She directed him to the highest point in the county where the panoramic night-time view glittered before them. Then he stopped the engine and stared out of the window for a few minutes before he spoke.

'Verity was a great friend of my wife's,' he explained. 'And through Kathy she became my friend, too. Then, when Kathy was diagnosed, I can't tell you how good she was to me and to Harriet.'

Sarah nodded. 'I don't need telling,' she said softly. 'I can believe it. She's one of the sweetest and kindest women I've ever met.'

Jamie nodded. 'So she is. And I think that I was rather blinded by her kindness and her beauty into believing that I was in love with her—'

'You don't have to say that, just to please me—'

He turned to face her then, his eyes blazing with emotion. 'But I'm not saying it just to please you, Sarah. I'm saying it because it happens to be true. It would have been so easy to have ended up with Verity—we were both lonely; we had children the same age and we got on well together. But. . .' and here he smiled, rather wistfully '. . .that isn't the same thing as love; not the same thing at all.' He wanted so badly to take Sarah into his arms but he forced himself to wait. He must tread very carefully here.

'Certainly it was nothing but a pale flame com-

pared to the blaze of passion I feel when I look at
you, Sarah—'

Sarah forced herself to ask questions that she
was afraid of hearing the answers to. 'And how
did you feel when you saw her tonight? Are you
saying that there was no pang? That you felt
nothing for her?'

He shook his head. 'How could I feel nothing
for someone who had been such a good friend? I
felt deep affection—nothing more.' He raised her
hand to his mouth and kissed it lingeringly. 'I want
to make love to you, Sarah.'

If she didn't ask, it would fester like a sore—
like it had been festering all night. 'Do you think
that's a good idea? Won't it remind you of making
love to Verity?'

How vulnerable she sounded, he thought. With
her voice stripped bare of all pretence and bravado.
'Darling,' he said protectively, 'I not only never
made love to Verity, I never even kissed her—not
properly.'

Sarah blinked, feeling as though the sun was
rising in her heart. 'Really?'

'Really.'

'Then why did you sever contact with her so
abruptly if there was nothing serious in it?'

He tried to explain what the situation had been
like. 'Because Verity and the kids and I had
become like a kind of insular little unit, which
wouldn't have worked with Benedict on the scene.
We decided that it would be best for all concerned
if we made a clean break of it, not realising, of

course—' and his eyes glimmered with reluctant amusement '—that I would fall in love with Ben's sister three years later.'

He took her hand and wrapped his own tightly round it. 'With hindsight, though, it was a bad thing for both girls—to sever all contact like that. But it was particularly bad for Harriet because she lost both Verity and Sammi so soon after losing her mother. In Harriet's eyes it must seem that all her father's relationships end in grief. I think that is what has made her so hostile towards you. She thinks that if she allows herself to grow fond of you then you'll be taken away from her. Like all the others.'

'And what's going to make her think otherwise?'

'Time. And patience. We talk to her. We explain things. We tell her that we'll always be there for her. We tell her we're in love—'

'We are?'

'Well, I know I am—how about you?' he murmured.

'Oh, Jamie,' said Sarah, her voice breaking. 'I've loved you from the moment I saw you!'

He stared at her hard for a long, long moment and when he spoke there was a question in his voice. 'I look at you now, my darling—so young and so vibrant and so beautiful—and I realise that I'm taking it all for myself—every last gorgeous thing about you. And wondering whether I deserve you.'

Sarah shook her head with a gentle smile. 'But

you're not taking,' she contradicted quietly. 'I'm giving. There is a difference, you know.'

'But I have a past,' he reminded her. 'A wife who died, a daughter who may take a while to accept you—'

'The past has made you the man you are today,' she told him simply. 'And that's the man I love. Nothing else matters other than that, Jamie.'

His blue eyes were soft. 'Are you pregnant?'

She shrugged. 'I don't think so. I'm not certain yet but I don't *feel* any different.'

'Some women don't,' he pointed out.

She smiled knowingly. 'Oh, but *I* will,' she said with heartfelt fervour and Jamie laughed.

'Somehow I believe you,' he whispered, but there was a lightness to his voice that made Sarah look at him closely.

'You're pleased I'm not pregnant.' It was a statement and not a question and he nodded, not flinching from telling her the truth but knowing in his heart that he could tell her anything now and that she would accept it.

'A little,' he admitted. 'Though on a practical level, rather than an emotional one. A new baby at this stage would only have complicated matters—certainly in Harriet's eyes.'

He pulled the pin out of her hair so that it fell around her face and he began stroking the dark, silken strands. 'We'll have to work hard to convince Harriet that she can be secure again,' he warned. 'And it isn't going to be easy.'

'I don't mind,' she whispered, her reply coming

straight from the heart. 'Really, I don't.'

The look in her eyes as she said it shook him to the very core and Jamie said a short prayer of thanks for whoever was responsible for allowing him to experience the kind of happiness he thought was lost to him for ever.

'Perhaps it's Kathy,' said Sarah, uncannily echoing his thoughts. 'She wants you to be happy, darling.'

There were questions that he, too, had been avoiding. 'Are you jealous of Kathy?'

She spoke with care. 'How could I be jealous of a woman who died? Kathy was your wife and the mother of your child. We need to keep her memory alive for Harriet's sake. So please don't worry—she'll always be a part of our family, Jamie.'

He let his head fall in his hands for a moment, too shaken with emotion to be able to speak, and when he looked up he saw that Sarah's eyes were very bright, too.

He let her cry for a moment or two, stroking her hair and whispering that he loved her over and over again in her ear, and when eventually she raised her head she was smiling.

'Thank you,' she gulped.

He shook his head. 'No, darling, thank *you*. For your understanding and your sweetness. You may be young and very beautiful but you have a wisdom which goes way, way beyond your years.' He tilted her chin and stared down at her. 'And I want you to know that I'll court you for however long you need before you'll marry me.'

'How long did you have in mind?' asked Sarah in alarm.

He shrugged. 'Whatever you decide. Some people consider a wait of two years to be appropriate.'

Two months was more in Sarah's time-scale but she would broach that tomorrow because right now Jamie seemed to have other things on his mind since he had pulled her with serious intent into his arms. He lifted his arm up behind her back to glance at his wristwatch.

'W-what are you doing?' she asked breathlessly.

'Seeing how long we've got left before we go back and announce our news. Good. Just over an hour. That should give us time.'

Something husky and determined in his voice had her quivering with excitement. 'Time for what?'

'*This*,' he growled.

And kissed her.

MILLS & BOON®

Weddings ♣ Glamour ♣ Family ♣ Heartbreak

Weddings By DeWilde

Since the turn of the century, the elegant and fashionable DeWilde stores have helped brides around the world realise the fantasy of their 'special day'.

Now the store and three generations of the DeWilde family are torn apart by the separation of Grace and Jeffrey DeWilde—and family members face new challenges and loves in this fast-paced, glamourous, internationally set series.

For weddings, romance and glamour, enter the world of

Weddings By DeWilde

—a fantastic line up of 12 new stories from popular Mills & Boon authors

NOVEMBER 1996

Bk. 3 DRESSED TO THRILL - Kate Hoffmann
Bk. 4 WILDE HEART - Daphne Clair

Available from WH Smith, John Menzies, Volume One, Forbuoys, Martins, Woolworths, Tesco, Asda, Safeway and other paperback stockists.

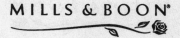

MILLS & BOON®

Back by Popular Demand

BETTY NEELS

COLLECTOR'S EDITION

A collector's edition of favourite titles from one of the world's best-loved romance authors.

Mills & Boon are proud to bring back these sought after titles, now reissued in beautifully matching volumes and presented as one cherished collection.

Don't miss these unforgettable titles, coming next month:

Title #13 COBWEB MORNING
Title #14 HENRIETTA'S OWN CASTLE

Available wherever
Mills & Boon books are sold

GET 4 BOOKS AND A MYSTERY GIFT

Return this coupon and we'll send you 4 Mills & Boon Medical Romance™ novels and a mystery gift absolutely FREE! We'll even pay the postage and packing for you.

We're making you this offer to introduce you to the benefits of Reader Service: FREE home delivery of brand-new Mills & Boon Medical Romance novels, at least a month before they are available in the shops, FREE gifts and a monthly Newsletter packed with information.

Accepting these FREE books and gift places you under no obligation to buy, you may cancel at any time, even after receiving just your free shipment. Simply complete the coupon below and send it to:

MILLS & BOON® READER SERVICE, FREEPOST, CROYDON, SURREY, CR9 3WZ.

No stamp needed

Yes, please send me 4 free Mills & Boon Medical Romance novels and a mystery gift. I understand that unless you hear from me, I will receive 4 superb new titles every month for just £2.10* each postage and packing free. I am under no obligation to purchase any books and I may cancel or suspend my subscription at any time, but the free books and gifts will be mine to keep in any case. (I am over 18 years of age)

M6JE

Ms/Mrs/Miss/Mr _____

Address _____

_____

_____ Postcode_____

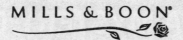

MILLS & BOON®

Medical Romance™

Books for enjoyment this month...

THE REAL FANTASY	Caroline Anderson
A LOVING PARTNERSHIP	Jenny Bryant
FOR NOW, FOR ALWAYS	Josie Metcalfe
TAKING IT ALL	Sharon Kendrick

Treats in store!

Watch next month for these absorbing stories...

THE IDEAL CHOICE	Caroline Anderson
A SURGEON'S CARE	Lucy Clark
THE HEALING TOUCH	Rebecca Lang
MORE THAN SKIN-DEEP	Margaret O'Neill

Available from:
W.H. Smith, John Menzies, Volume One, Forbuoys, Martins,
Woolworths, Tesco, Asda, Safeway and other paperback stockists.

Readers in South Africa - write to:
IBS, Private Bag X3010, Randburg 2125.